Accosting the Golden Spire

Iris Weil Collett

Throughout the usual work of accountants, there is the constant pressure to follow the principles of GAAP. Audit procedures are prescribed and due adherence to the rules will produce statements of historical results and current fiscal condition, which meet all the criteria.

— Melvin I. Shapiro, CPA

THOMAS HORTON AND DAUGHTERS
26662 S. New Town Drive / Sun Lakes, AZ 85248

Dedicated to
Anna, Dianna, and Yvonne

Accosting the Golden Spire is fiction, and all the characters and adventures are imaginary. Any resemblance to actual persons, living or dead, is purely coincidental.

Library of Congress Catalog Card Number 88-82327

ISBN Number 0-913878-43-X

PREFACE

A supplementary text to be used near the end of a principles of accounting course or at the beginning of an Intermediate Accounting course. Would be ideal for a MBA program which has a light coverage of accounting. Could be used in CPA firms' in-house training programs.

Mixes fraud, crime, ethics, and accounting together to get a better way of learning the accounting process. If used as a supplement to an accounting course or a public finance course, this gripping and at times humorous novel provides a painless way of learning many accounting and finance principles. This suspenseful novel puts accounting concepts into words a novice can understand and enjoy. Since much of the plot is in foreign countries, the book could be used in an introductory international accounting or finance course.

Lenny Cramer, a professor at Wharton's School of Finance, operates a small forensic accounting firm. He teaches, testifies before Congress, and appears as an expert witness in a court battle. The real action occurs when he investigates fraud in a friend's jade shop. This investigative accountant uncovers a plot to steal treasures from a socialistic Asian country.

Featuring a sleuth and a con-man who handle balance sheets and income statements and financial records the way most detectives handle guns, the humorous characters put accounting and business concepts into real-life individual and business decisions. Along the way business practices and political controversies, contemporary individual and corporate planning, tax fraud and avoidance, and the dynamic and exciting life of CPAs and financial consultants are elucidated in a way both students and instructors will find gripping as well as informative.

The novel approach is an excellent substitution for a dull practice set, and is a flexible teaching tool to overcome boredom in the classroom. The concepts and attitudes a novel teaches last long after the facts are gone.

CHAPTER 1

> I'm not sure I'm the fall guy in that sense of the word. As far as spears in the breast are concerned, I don't mind spears in the breast. It's knives in the back that concern me.
>
> — Donald T. Regan

Frank Harrison liked to dress in white clothes. To him, white clothes went best with his dark features, and at the same time, conveyed a sense of freshness and an aura of serenity. As he looked at himself in the mirror, he was pleased by the appearance of his white linen double-breasted suit with no vents and double-pleated full slacks. It would feel cool in the sweltering summer heat outside.

White clothing has a subtle appeal of luxury and worldliness which dates back to the days when dry cleaning was inaccessible to the masses. Frank liked this feeling of superiority. He also felt that wearing white gave him an edge on those individuals who met him for the first time.

"That woman had better be ready," he muttered to himself as he lit a cigarette and took a long drag.

Frank hated being late and hated being kept waiting even more. He glanced at his watch. 7:42. Plenty of time to get to Angela's by 8:10 and Mellinis at 9:00 for his dinner reservation.

Frank loved seafood risotto — especially the way Mellinis prepared it. They used genuine arborio short-grain Italian rice from the Po Valley of Italy. It plumped up and became creamy when cooked in chicken broth, but the rice must be stirred constantly with a wooden spoon over consistent medium heat. Otherwise it will stick. Mellinis prepared it just right and served it with clams, mussels, and shrimp.

"There," he said, placing a red boutonniere in his lapel. Another glance at his watch. 7:46. "Time to leave," he thought to himself, picking up the lit cigarette before he went out the door of his Center City townhouse.

"Rats! I'll kill the mutt!" he said as he stepped in some dog excrement outside his house. He threw his cigarette down in disgust and began dragging his right white leather shoe along the sidewalk. Frank spotted a little patch of green grass across Front Street and began to wipe his right shoe on the grass to remove the excrement.

"Good-for-nothing dog," he muttered as he walked to his car.

It was now 7:49 and Frank knew it took only fifteen minutes to get to Angela's place. He started to relax.

As Frank began to cross the street to go to his car, he suddenly heard a splash. Too late to jump away, he was sprayed with dirty water when a passing van drove through a puddle of water in the street.

"No!" he raged as he pounded his right fist on the hood of a parked light blue Chevrolet that was also dripping with dirty water from the splash. Frank stared down at his trousers and saw the effects of the splash. His jacket was stained as well as his shirt. Only his red boutonniere escaped unscathed.

Furious, Frank walked back to his house to change. He knew that he would undoubtedly be late for his date with Angela and that just infuriated him more.

As he approached his house he saw a brown cocker spaniel beginning to raise its leg against his door. Frank became incensed.

"You, you're the cause for all this," he thought to himself. "I'll fix you," he muttered.

With an insincere smile, Frank approached the dog slowly, being careful where he stepped to avoid a repeat of his previous predicament. In a sweet tone he said to the dog, "Hi, fella. How're you doing? You're a good dog."

The dog looked up at Frank with big brown eyes and began to wag its tail as Frank approached.

"That's a good dog. Would you like to come inside with your friend, Frank?" he asked.

The dog tilted its head to the side, tail still wagging, looking at him.

"Come on, come on, fella. Come on in, fella. It's okay. Frank's got something nice for you. There you go. It's okay," Frank said, opening the door.

After staring for what seemed to be the longest time, the cocker spaniel went into Frank's home, carefully sniffing the floor as it entered.

Frank immediately walked to his kitchen. "I've got something special for you," he said, opening his refrigerator door.

He pulled out a little piece of ground beef and said, "Here you are, fella. It's okay."

Frank laid the beef on the floor near the dog. The dog began to sniff at the beef. Then it carefully licked a little bit of the ground beef to decide if it was desirable. Finding the beef appealing, the dog soon ate it and began to wag its tail quickly.

"Good boy!" exclaimed Frank. "Do you want some more? Here you are."

This time the dog ate it out of Frank's hand. It was clear that the dog was beginning to both like and trust Frank.

"How would you like to take a nice warm bath? That's a good boy! Come on! Come on, fella," Frank said, walking up the stairs.

The cocker spaniel, confident that it had found a new friend and possible master, dutifully followed Frank up the stairs.

* * *

As he looked at himself again in the mirror, Frank began to calm down. He was about six-foot-one and one hundred sixty-five pounds with dark hair. He was certainly not the type of man who was physically imposing, but he had a sleek look about him. He also believed he had a certain smoothness about him that made him irresistible to women.

Frank began to turn his attention to Angela. He checked his watch. 8:20. He decided to call her on the phone and let her know that he was going to be late.

"Angela? This is Frank. I got a little tied up with something here, but I am leaving in about five minutes. I should be there around twenty of nine."

"Okay, Frank," said Angela. "What time is your dinner reservation?"

"Nine o'clock. We might have to rush a little, but we should make it."

"Okay, see you in a few minutes, Frank. Bye."

"Bye."

Frank again placed the red boutonniere in his white lapel. "It isn't as nice as my other white suit," he thought to himself, looking in the mirror, "but it'll do. Besides, I'm late."

Frank quickly headed for the door. As he left his house he glanced at his watch. 8:25. He should be able to get to Angela's by 8:40 if nothing went wrong.

This time Frank made it to his white Mazda 380 ZX without incident. Traffic was rather light for this time of night in Philadelphia, and Frank began to make good time in driving to Angela's South Philadelphia rowhouse. In Philadelphia, the downtown portion of eastbound Chestnut and westbound Walnut Streets are open only to buses and pedestrians between seven in the morning and seven at night. Since it was after eight at night Frank decided to proceed west on Walnut from his Front Street address. As he approached Fifth and Walnut, he glanced to his right and could see police barricades two blocks north around Fifth and Market. Independence Hall, the Liberty Bell, and many other historical sites were being decorated in anticipation of the arrival of a number of tourists for Philadelphia's annual Fourth of July celebration in a few weeks. He was glad that he would be back from his trip to the Far East in time for the festivities.

Frank knew that the traffic lights were timed on both Chestnut and Walnut Streets so he drove between 25 and 30 miles per hour. Hopefully, he would not have to stop for a red light the entire way. Frank was making very good time since most of the businesses in Center City Philadelphia closed down at night except for restaurants, movies and theaters. He continued to drive past many closed stores on the largely barren streets that were well lit by the bright street lights shaped like old-fashioned gas lamps. Suddenly, Frank decided to turn north on Tenth Street in order to pass by the jade shop of which he was a part owner.

The shop was located on Sansom Street, which is a small side street between the major arteries of Chesnut and Walnut Street. This section of Sansom Street was known as "Jeweler's Row" because of the large number of jewelry shops located in this area. Prior to the construction of suburban shopping malls, anyone purchasing jewelry in the metropolitan Philadelphia area either shopped at Jeweler's Row or bought jewelry at an excellent discount because of "the low overhead" from the trunk of an automobile from a guy named Lefty who was known around the neighborhood as a dealer of hot merchandise. While business was not quite as good as it had been in its heyday, many Philadelphians still came to Sansom Street to shop because the huge selection of jewelry stores in a concentrated area enabled most customers to find whatever they were seeking.

Even though jade was a sideline for Frank, his knowledge of jade was highly regarded among those in the profession. Frank's main line of business was his consulting firm, Quaker City Consulting, Inc. His firm did a great deal of consulting for many prominent businesses in the city. He competed with many national and regional CPA firms. Since Quaker City Consulting was one of the largest consulting firms in Philadelphia, Frank had many contacts throughout the city.

Frank was a little concerned when he formed the partnership with Dana Scott. Through a mutual friend they discovered that they were both bidding to buy the same jade shop. Frank called Dana and told her, "We need to be in partnership together. A partnership's income is taxed only once as part of the owner's share of income in the business. A corporation's income is taxed twice — once at the corporate level as part of corporate income, and again at the stockholder level as a tax on dividend income." He was able to talk Dana into a partnership, Frank suspected, because Dana was short of working capital.

Frank wanted to make sure that Dana Scott was a responsible person before he entered into a partnership agreement. Frank knew that in a partnership, mutual agency exists, which means that if one partner signs an agreement involving the partnership, the other partner is just as responsible for the agreement as the one who physically signs. He did not know if Dana realized it, but a partnership with an irresponsible individual could lead to financial disaster. Unlike in a corporation where there is limited liability to the owners (one can only lose one's original investment in most cases), a partnership provides unlimited liability to the owners.

Frank's investigation of Dana Scott convinced him that she was an intelligent, responsible businessperson with whom he could deal. To be on the safe side, however, Frank placed many of his personal assets in the name of Quaker City Consultants to limit his liability should something unforeseen occur with the partnership. He knew that Dana was unaware of these transactions.

All was peaceful around his jade shop as he drove by and saw the metal cage around the front window. Almost all retailers in this area had such cages in front of their windows to guard against theft and vandalism after closing.

His thoughts were interrupted as he turned back onto Walnut and continued west until he turned south on Broad Street. Broad Street was Frank's favorite street in Philadelphia. His consulting firm was located just a block north of here at Broad and Chestnut. City Hall was one block north of it at Broad and Market. In reality, Broad Street should be Fourteenth Street (in

Philadelphia the numbered streets run north and south], but the number fourteen had been skipped. But without question, it is the major street in Philadelphia. It runs the entire length of the city in an almost complete straight line with City Hall directly in the middle at Broad and Market Streets. Market Street is the dividing line between north and south in the city.

With City Hall as large as life in his rearview mirror, Frank saw that Broad Street was already decorated for Independence Day. Flags were hanging from wires above the street and red, white, and blue bunting was wrapped around the light poles. Soon, on his right, he saw the foreboding image of the Union League at Broad and Spruce. The Union League was an organization that was exclusively male until the mid-1980s and was headquartered in an old red stone building shaped like a castle, with various flags hanging outside its windows. Just about every important Philadelphia businessman and politician was a member. Frank was, and he saw many business decisions and political deals made on its premises.

"Watch it, you jerk!" he yelled as a yellow taxi with an advertisement for an Atlantic City casino on its roof swerved in front of him.

Frank continued south on Broad and began to enter some more residential areas. Trees became more visible as Frank began to pass rowhouse after rowhouse much like the blue-collar area where he had grown up in Southwest Philadelphia. Frank began to think about Angela. This was his first date with her. Angela was the type of girl he liked: 24 and a high school graduate. Frank liked girls who were not too bright, because he felt they were easier to intimidate.

Frank was not interested in a serious romance with any woman. He had been married six months — fifteen years ago. He was distrustful of women ever since his mother left his father when Frank was only twelve. He preferred instead to win over any pretty face he saw just for the night and not worry about tomorrow. He saw women as sexual objects with the ability to handle some domestic work. But Frank Harrison was smart enough to keep his opinion of women as private as possible, and as a good businessman he made exceptions. After all, he did have a woman as a business partner.

He had slipped on one occasion when he was taking a night course at Drexel University many years ago. Each participant had to prepare a project explaining why productivity had declined over the last twenty years. Harrison prepared two illustrations. One was labeled the 1950s and showed a woman barefoot and pregnant. The other was labeled the 1980s and showed a woman in a business suit.

As he parked his car in front of Angela's house, Frank was pleased. Normally it is very difficult to find a place to park in many of the residential neighborhoods of Philadelphia. Not only was Frank able to find a place to park, but it was right in front of Angela's house. He felt the night just might turn out to be successful after all. It was 8:37 and they had an excellent chance to make their dinner reservation. He could taste the seafood risotto.

Frank walked up the steps to Angela's rowhome and rang the bell. Like thousands of other rowhomes in Philadelphia, one had to walk up three steps to reach the doorway of the three-story brick structure. As was typical of many South Philadelphia neighborhoods, many people were sitting out on the steps in front of their homes talking to their neighbors or watching what was going on along the street.

"Hi, Angela, you ready?"

"Hi, Frank. No, not yet. Why don't you come in and wait?"

"All right."

Frank was seething. "How could she not be ready?" he said to himself. He took out a cigarette and began to smoke.

"Do you think you'll be much longer?" Frank asked, looking at his Rolex, which now indicated that it was 8:42.

"About five more minutes. There's beer in the refrigerator if you're thirsty."

"You know we have a reservation at 9:00 at Mellinis."

"I shouldn't be much longer."

Frank began to pace. "That idiot," he thought to himself, growing more and more impatient by the minute, "she's not good looking enough to take this long."

It was now 8:45. Frank estimated that it took 20 to 25 minutes to get to Mellinis from Angela's house. He took a long puff from his cigarette.

"Maybe I should call the restaurant and tell them we are going to be late."

"Whatever you think is best, Frank. I'm going to be only a few more minutes."

Frank picked up the phone and called Mellinis.

"Good evening, Mellinis Restaurant, this is Vito. May I help you?"

"Yes, my name is Harrison. I have a reservation for two at 9:00, and we're running a little late. Will there be a problem with my reservation?"

"Well, sir, our policy is to hold our reservations for ten minutes before we open up your table. We are particularly busy tonight, so I do not think we will be able to hold your table beyond 9:10."

Frank looked at his watch. 8:49. "Is it possible to change my reservation to a later seating?"

"I am very sorry, sir, but our only other seating this evening is 9:45 and we are booked solid at that time."

"Surely you can do something for me! I am one of your best customers."

"Believe me, Mr. Harrison, I would like to help you out, but it is not possible. We are booked solid. There is nothing I can do."

Frank began to get angry. Frank liked to think of himself as a bigshot. He did not like it when people did not try to give him special privileges. He also felt that he could intimidate Vito.

"I don't think you understand. I'm Frank Harrison. I have dinner at your restaurant three or four times a month. Do you expect me to believe that there is nothing you can do for me?"

"It is out of my hands, Mr. Harrison. If you would like, I can get our manager, Mr. Orsini, to talk with you."

"Yes, get him," Frank shouted.

Frank looked at his watch. It was now 8:52 and Angela was still upstairs. "What in the world could be taking her so long?" he wondered. Before he had any more time to get angry with Angela, a voice came over the phone.

"Hello, this is Ray Orsini, may I help you?"

"This is Frank Harrison and I have a reservation for 9:00 that I would like to have either held for me or changed to 9:45."

"Mr. Harrison, the best I can do for you is to hold your reservation until 9:10. We have a very large crowd this evening and I cannot possibly hold your reservation beyond that time."

"I have dinner at your restaurant at least three or four times a month. Is this how you treat loyal customers?"

"I would like to help you, Mr. Harrison, but it is not possible. I am sorry."

"You are no better than your peon Vito. How can you treat good customers this way? Didn't you ever hear of goodwill?"

"I know all about goodwill, sir, that is why — "

"You don't know a single thing about goodwill. Goodwill is the value of establishing a good name. In accounting, goodwill is an amortizable asset that is the excess of the purchase price of an entity over the sum of the fair values of all its identifiable assets less its liabilities. You people seem to be trying to create negative goodwill by establishing a reputation that you show no favoritism for your good customers."

"I'm sorry you feel that way, Mr. Harrison. We appreciate your patronage, but there is nothing I can do tonight."

"Fine." With that Frank slammed down the phone and began muttering to himself, "I'll fix those haughty blue bloods."

Frank was very sensitive about his blue-collar background. Frank's father was an electrician in a General Electric plant in Southwest Philadelphia where Frank was born and raised, and unlike many of his clients and business associates, Frank had to work his way through school at Temple University. Many people he dealt with professionally respected Frank for his business capabilities, but it took time. Initially, he had been passed over by potential clients who had gone to Ivy League schools — like the University of Pennsylvania's Wharton School or other prominent private schools like Villanova University located in Philadelphia's exclusive Main Line — because they felt that Frank's bachelor's degree from Temple and MBA from Drexel University did not qualify him to do high-level consulting. Frank had to work harder than others in order to establish himself as a well-respected consultant.

Although he was now very successful, snide comments were still made about both his alma mater and his socioeconomic background. Frank knew that many of his clients felt that he did not have the so-called "proper breeding," and try as he might to ignore it, he was still bothered by it. Frank did find some solace in knowing that many of these rich snobs paid him good money for his Temple University knowledge, rather than hiring another firm composed entirely of Wharton graduates. Nonetheless, Frank always remained suspicious of those who considered themselves among the upper crust of society.

"Hi."

Frank turned around. Finally Angela was ready. She was smiling. The expression in her dark brown eyes indicated that she was oblivious to everything else in the world except how she looked to Frank. She wanted to be complimented. "They all do," he thought, but Frank was not in the mood for paying compliments.

"Well, I hope you're happy. Because you are so late we missed our dinner reservation. Now what are we going to do for dinner?"

"I'm sorry, Frank, but I didn't know."

"What do you mean you didn't know! I told you we had a dinner reservation at 9:00."

"I forgot, but you were the one who was late. You even called."

"Listen, moron, I know I was late, but when I got here you still were not ready."

Frank was extremely angry now. How dare she try to blame him for being late. He took a deep breath and looked at her. She obviously was astonished at being spoken to in the tone of voice Frank used. It was clear she did not like being called a moron. At this point, Frank did not care. She was not as attractive as he had thought she was when he first met her at a Center City bar the previous night. The darkness of the bar and the drinks he'd had must have made her more appealing to him than she was here in the bright light. But he did have to admit that she had a nice figure.

"I won't have some old man talk to me like that," said Angela in a trembling voice. "Get out and take your smelly cigarette smoke with you."

Angela had struck a nerve. Frank was thirty-eight years old but he felt that he looked twenty-seven. He worked hard at maintaining a youthful appearance by working out daily at the spa and using the tanning machine. He loved to boast to people that he had the same size waist he had had in ninth grade. To have Angela call him old was more than he could tolerate.

"Who are you calling old, moron?"

Angela, in a combination of screaming and crying, shrieked, "Get out! Get out now!"

"Fine! You want me to leave? No problem. I'm out of here, baby, but no one talks to Frank Harrison like that and gets away with it." Frank rarely used the pronoun I, preferring to always use his name as a form of self-promotion.

As Frank went towards the front door, he noticed a small glass vase sitting on a fragile looking end table by the door. As he went out the door Frank slammed it hard enough to hear the windows vibrate and a crashing sound of the vase hitting the floor above the sound of Angela's screaming voice.

"No!" Angela shouted as she began to sob uncontrollably.

As Frank got into his car he could hear two elderly women out on their step talking.

"I wonder if this one beat up poor Angela."

"He looks like the type who would like to hit women, Rita. You can never trust men with white suits unless they look like Caesar Romero."

Frank pivoted toward the women quickly and in an angry voice said, "For your information, ladies, I didn't touch her, but sometimes I get a kick out of slapping old busybodies around."

The women recoiled and quickly went inside the house. They watched Frank through the venetian blind as he drove away.

* * *

Halfway through his drive home Frank calmed down enough to think about his trip to Burma. He wanted to study the Burmese government before his trip. He decided that he would stop at his consulting office to pick up some maps and books on Burma and spend part of the evening reading at home.

* * *

"What?" mumbled Armando Mellini. Then he recognized that it was the telephone. It was two-fifteen in the morning. "Who could be calling at this time? I hope everything is all right," he thought to himself.

"Hello, Mr. Mellini," said the voice on the other end of the phone. "This is ABD Security Systems. The alarm has gone off in your restaurant. We have already notified the Philadelphia police. They said they would send a car around immediately."

"Thank you. I'll be there right away."

"Who was that? Is Uncle Giuseppe okay?"

"It was the security company. They said that the burglar alarm went off in the restaurant," Mellini said to his wife as he began to get dressed. "I'm going over there and see what happened."

"You be careful, Armando."

"Don't worry, my dear. The police are on their way. You go back to sleep now. See you."

As Mellini got into his car he thought how glad he was that he had listened to his accountant's advice and signed a contract with the security company.

"The cost of having a good security system is an operating expense just like the salaries expense you have for your employees, the cost of utilities, the depreciation deduction on your kitchen appliances and dining room tables, and the amortization of your food and liquor licenses," his accountant had told him.

"They are all necessary expenses your business incurs in its day-to-day operations. It is not like the accounting classification of other personal expenses which are not associated with your restaurant business, or like extraordinary items which result from unusual, non-recurring, material events, such as loss from the condemnation of a building. The expense of paying each month to have a good burglar alarm system in operation is something I would not hesitate to incur."

His accountant had helped Mellini with other things as well. He helped establish a good internal control system by separating duties which made it more difficult for employees to steal from Mellini. One such control was to have the waiters and waitresses bring the bill to a cashier who rang up the bill on the cash register and gave whatever change there was to the waiters and waitresses. The cashier then kept all the lunch and dinner checks.

The checks had to be initialed by three people: the chef, to indicate that he received the order; the waiter or waitress, to indicate that the order was paid for; and the cashier, to indicate that the bill was rung up. Each customer order had four copies: one for the customer; one to be controlled by the chef in the kitchen; one to be kept by the waiter or waitress; and one to be retained by the cashier.

At the end of the day, the manager would reconcile the three sets of customer orders with the day's cash receipts to help insure that cash was not being stolen from Mellini and that meals were not being given away without proper authorization. Since the establishment of this system of internal control, cash receipts had increased by five percent and inventory shrinkage had decreased by eight percent.

The implementation of a petty cash system by the helpful accountant had worked also. A petty cash system is a record-keeping system for small cash disbursements typically associated with an office. Some items, such as postage, had to be paid immediately in cash. In a typical petty cash system, a certain amount (generally small) of cash is placed in a cash box. Each time cash is needed for small expenditures (i.e., postage, cab fare, newspapers, etc.), the individual authorized to control the petty cash writes a voucher explaining what the cash is to be used for. This voucher is later supplemented by a receipt for the purchase of the item or service (i.e., a cab ride). When the cash is replenished, the documents are typically reconciled to determine if all the cash is accounted for. Once this is completed, the transactions that used up the petty cash, such as postage and taxis, are recorded as expenses in the general journal.

The petty cash fund helped Mellini know how some of his cash was being spent for things around his office. This worked a lot better than Betty coming to him asking for twelve dollars to pay UPS and then not having any record of it later. Many expenses went unrecognized, causing income to be overstated. Every minor two-dollar expense did not have to be recorded each time it occurred, either. Instead, the lump sum of the petty cash expenditures could be recorded in the aggregate when petty cash was replenished. At times, Mellini suspected that some people might have asked him for cash that was greater than the amount of the expense. By having a formalized system of keeping track of the petty cash, Mellini was spared the responsibility of having to remember to make a note of the expense. All in all, Mellini was pleased with the work his accountant had done for him.

Mellini did not have any problem parking his car on Passyunk Avenue at this time of night, and was relieved to see that the police were already there. He had heard stories about how long it sometimes takes for the Philadelphia police to respond to calls, but they were already at the South Philadelphia restaurant close to the Philadelphia Sports Complex.

"Excuse me, officer, but I'm Armando Mellini. I own this restaurant."

"Could I see some identification, Mr. Mellini?"

Mellini pulled out his wallet and took out his driver's license. "Here you are, officer."

The police officer looked at the name on the license, then the picture. The picture was a reasonable likeness considering that it was a driver's license photo. Mellini was 44 and had a round face with dark eyes and a swarthy complexion. His dark bushy hair was beginning to recede. His nose and ears were disproportionately large for his face. What the picture failed to reveal was the four-inch scar Mellini had behind his ear as a result of an accident he suffered while in the Air Force, and his rotund diminutive style. At a quick glance he could look like the actor, Danny DeVito, except that Mellini was taller at five foot eight inches tall.

The officer looked at Mellini and returned the license to him.

"There you are, Mr. Mellini. I'm Officer Mulrooney. It looks like an act of vandalism. Your front window was broken but nothing appears to have been taken. Officer Hawkins and I inspected the interior and everything seems to be in order, but you ought to have a look for yourself before we file a report."

After spending fifteen minutes looking through the restaurant, Mellini was satisfied that nothing was taken. All the tables with their respective red and white checkered tablecloths were in place. The cash register was neither damaged nor open. Mellini's accountant had instituted a system whereby the evening's cash receipts were always dropped off in an overnight depository at the bank to limit the likelihood of theft. The kitchen and barroom areas were untouched. The autographed pictures in the lobby of Frank Sinatra, Enzo Stuarti, Tony Martin, Dean Martin, Tony Bennett, and Eddie Fisher were not damaged either. The only damage was the broken front window, which needed to be replaced. Glass also needed to be swept up.

"I do not understand why someone would do something like this," Mellini said to Mulrooney. "This is generally a safe neighborhood. My father started this restaurant forty-seven years ago. People come here — they eat, they enjoy. They come before Phillies games, they come after Phillies games. Now this! In all the time my family's been here, there has never been nothing like this. Why now? It serves no point."

"Normally it's just some kids who are looking for trouble, although the ones who did this to your window must be real sick."

"Why do you say that?"

"Normally," Mulrooney said, "broken windows like this are caused by someone throwing a brick or a stone or a beer bottle. Something along those lines. But in all my eight years on the force, I've never seen anyone use what was used to break your window tonight: a brick tied to a dead cocker spaniel."

"You mean a dog?" inquired the astonished Mellini.

"Yeah, do you know anyone who would do this to you? A disgruntled employee or someone you fired recently?"

"No one," replied Mellini pensively.

"I hope you don't take offense at this question, Mr. Mellini, but have you had any problems with the mob? Could they be threatening you?" inquired Mulrooney.

"No! Absolutely not!"

"Throwing a dead cocker spaniel through a window is not the way the mob generally operates," conceded Mulrooney. "Most likely it was just some kids. Murphy, have someone take that dog to Penn's vet school. I want to see how that dog died. We might be able to find something out about the perpetrator this way. Mr. Mellini, I'm going to have you fill out a couple of forms and then you can get to the task of covering up your window and going back home to bed."

"I still can't get over it," stated a bewildered Mellini, "a dead cocker spaniel. Who would do such a cruel thing? Even Hitler liked animals."

CHAPTER 2

The requirement that inventory be recorded at its historical cost is modified in one situation. When the market value of the inventory falls below cost, the inventory should be written down to its market value and the corresponding loss should be included in the income statement.
— Nikolai, Bazley, and Stallman

A Thai plane descended through clear skies, crossing the Gulf of Martaban and the Bay of Bengal en route to landing in Rangoon, Burma, in several minutes. This landing could not be as frightening as landing in Hong Kong, thought Lenny as he awoke when the woman seated next to him touched his arm. His two previous flights into Hong Kong had prepared him for anything. The planes bank steeply over high-rise buildings and straighten out just in time to land on a large pier at Kai Tak airport.

But Hong Kong, the freckle on the face of Asia, was behind him. He had found the city to be an exuberant mix of high fashion, high finance, deluxe hotels, and traditional Chinese culture.

Lenny hurriedly stood up from his aisle seat, and retrieved his empty mineral water bottle from the overhead compartment. He walked back to a petite Thai hostess who filled up his bottle. When he got back to Row 18, seat C, Rebecca, his daughter, was engaged in a conversation with the woman sitting in the middle seat.

Safe mineral water was essential for the next four days in Burma. He and Rebecca had survived China without getting the dreaded diarrhea or "Delhi Belly." They had followed several rules: 1) don't drink untreated water, 2) peel all fruit, 3) don't eat or drink dairy products, and 4) eat only cooked vegetables.

What had the guide book said? You will get sick in Asia. The bacteria in Asian water and food is different from that in American food. He and Rebecca had drunk a lot of soft drinks in China.

Their Thai guide who met them in the Bangkok airport earlier certainly had not been encouraging. Prawit Chareonkul casually mentioned that the next four days would be rugged. He handed each of the eleven tourists in his group five or six towelets. They said "With the Compliments of Diethelm Travel. Your Guide to Unusual Places: 544 Ploenchit Road, Bangkok, Thailand." For some reason the name of the travel agency had made Lenny think again about diarrhea.

"Use these; it will be hot," Prawit calmly spoke. "Our rooms may not have air conditioning. You'll have rats running around your room, and roaches may crawl over your face during the night. The plumbing may not work." There were some strange looks on the tour group faces.

Prawit then suggested, "Go to the shop over there and buy several cartons of cigarettes. You can use them for trading and for tips in Burma."

The ageless and likable U.S. tour director, Joan Kelley, shot back, "We've already paid for our tips." She always looked after her "children," which was how she thought of her tour group.

Typical of non-smoking Americans, several of the tour members mumbled that they would not be a party to killing foreigners by giving them cigarettes. Only one man heeded Prawit's first important advice.

Another male tour member asked, "What is the exchange rate in Burma?"

Prawit responded, "7 to 1."

"Is there a black market rate?"

"Yes. About 25 or 30 to 1."

"Is it safe to exchange money on the black market?"

"No," was Prawit's response. "Burma has a socialistic-military government. Much of the country is controlled by General Maung Maung, a dictator."

The entire dialogue caused Lenny to chuckle to himself as he thought of the impact an economic climate like Burma's would have on accounting. Assets, for example, include all costs necessary to make the asset operational. Consequently, the cost of a machine would include not only the purchase price of the machine itself, but also costs such as installation and shipping. Measurement of the cost is relatively easy since everything is in dollars. In Burma, however, there would be the purchase price plus the cost of cartons of cigarettes to bribe individuals to deliver the machine.

"What a nightmare!" he thought to himself as he tried to determine in his own mind if a gain should be recognized on the cartons of cigarettes when they were traded to reflect their increased market value over their original cost. Lenny decided that a gain would be recognized on the disposal of the cigarettes if their market value was determinable. Otherwise, the cost of the asset would simply equal the acquisition price and the cost of the cigarettes plus items needed to make the asset operational.

Lenny's train of thought was broken by Rebecca's voice. "Dad! Dad! Come in world." She reached over the woman in the middle seat, grabbed Lenny's arm and said, "Dana's from Philadelphia also. She has a gem shop. Look at her beautiful ruby drop."

Lenny glanced over for the first time and looked at the large ruby on the woman between him and his daughter. His eyes moved downward slightly, but he immediately looked up into the blue eyes of Dana Scott. She turned in her seat to take Lenny's hand. He blushed slightly.

"Hello, Dr. Cramer; my name is Dana Scott. Your daughter has told me a lot about you. Did you enjoy your short nap?"

"Well, I'm not sure I went to sleep. Maybe I dozed."

"Rebecca says that you are an accountant. That's certainly not my cup of tea. Do you teach or practice accounting?"

"Both. I teach at Wharton's and also have a small accounting firm." At that moment the plane touched down at the Rangoon airport. "Where is your gem shop located?"

"Oh, I bought out another gentleman last year. It's located on jewelers row — Sansom Street. I own about 70% of it, and another partner owns the remainder. He's sitting back in the smoking section. I had to dump a quarter of a million into the shop. Are you with the Joan Kelley tour group?"

"Yes."

"Great, my friend and I" — Dana pointed to a woman in seat D — "joined the tour for Burma and Bali."

Dana leaned over Lenny and said, "Janet, this is Professor Cramer. He teaches accounting at Wharton's School of Finance. Maybe we should get him to tell us where all of our cash is going."

A sparkle from the ruby drop caught Lenny's eye, and he imagined that it was winking at him. She was so close he could smell her perfume. Lenny turned to his right and saw a smiling, chubby redhead. To both Janet and Dana he said, "Please, call me Lenny." Janet was wearing a jade necklace and a wide jade bracelet.

For some reason the plane had stopped on the runway. Feeling an overwhelming desire to continue the conversation, Lenny turned back to Dana and said, "So you're having cash flow problems? Tell me about your inventory. How often do you turn over your gem inventory?"

"Whoa! Talk to Janet. She's my bookkeeper. I don't know a debit from a credit. Would you like to get together this evening after we arrive at the Strand Hotel? You know there are no nightclubs in Rangoon, and dancing is not permitted in public places."

Lenny instinctively looked at his Cartier watch. It was 5:15. "I don't know. Rebecca needs to get her beauty sleep."

"Oh, come on, Dad. I'm 13 years old. I'm not a kid. We can

eat supper with Dana and Janet. There's nothing on T.V. There probably won't be a T.V."

The plane finally reached the airport entrance and everyone jumped up before the seat belt light went off. Lenny smiled, "Okay, we'll think about it."

Rebecca looked at Dana and smiled too, "That means yes."

Once inside the Mingaladon airport, the passport game was relatively easy. The eleven-member tour group met the local Burmese guide, who led the group outside where the hassle began. About 50 kids of all ages surrounded the group. First, they begged for the orchids which the women had received on the Thai plane. They wanted the safety pin attached to the back of the orchid. Then they began begging for paper, books, money, or anything they saw in purses or hand-carried luggage. They were all skinny and dirty.

Finally all eleven pieces of luggage were located and placed on the bus, and everyone climbed aboard. Each person was limited to one piece of luggage. It was still hot at 6:30. Someone demanded that the air conditioner be turned on, but it didn't work.

Lenny was in the back of the bus and Rebecca was sitting two seats in front with Dana. Lenny noticed that there was a distinct lack of high-rise buildings and modern automobiles in Rangoon. Apparently Burma had been isolated from the influences of the outside world. No one was rushing around, and there were no neon signs. He could vividly see neglect, decay, and lack of upkeep. Surprisingly, the streets were wide and were planned on a properly British colonial grid system.

Lenny's thoughts were interrupted by the voice of the local guide. "Rangoon has been the capital of Burma since 1885. Rangoon is located in the fertile delta country in south Burma — situated on the wide Rangoon River. A city with a population of about three million stands 30 kilometers above sea level. In 1885 the British conquered upper Burma, and the Burmese kingdom ended. Let me cover — "

Lenny saw Rebecca talking and gesturing to Dana. Lenny chuckled to himself. Rebecca Lea Cramer. Going into the seventh grade. A dirty blond, slender, athletic looking. She had beaten the boys in physical fitness tests in the fifth grade. Tanned, with a sprinkle of freckles on her nose, she was growing out of her tomboy stage into a young lady. She was the youngest of his three children, but her self-assurance and grown-up behavior made her appear to be 14 or 15.

Rebecca's mother had died only eleven months ago. A swift but painful death. The after-effects were more painful to Lenny than to Rebecca. He now had a housekeeper, who was only a partial substitute for a mother. The housekeeper was *no* substitute for a wife. This extra stress created what his doctor called "fatigue syndrome" — a mysterious yuppie disease. Many of its victims were young, white professionals. Lenny had developed headaches and sensitivity to light. Something was draining his physical strength and mental energy. His doctor suggested a vacation.

He had seen a flier on a campus bulletin board advertising an Asian study tour. The small ad was partly covered by a large brochure advertising a CPA review course. He called Joan Kelley, a marketing professor. Apparently she had taken about 15 trips throughout the world. He made a reservation for Rebecca and himself, but almost canceled when it came time to pay money. It had not been a vacation so far. There was a difference between a vacation and a trip. A trip was much more demanding. "But demanding as it might be," thought Lenny, "it was pleasant to spend some quality time with Rebecca, and more than pleasant to be in the company of an interesting woman such as Dana."

The bus stopped at 92 Strand Road in front of the Strand Hotel. Prawit indicated that dinner was scheduled for 7:30 and breakfast the next morning from 7:00 to 8:00. The tour group would leave for Shwedagon Pagoda at 8:00.

Both the hotel and its furniture were old, but the room that Lenny and Rebecca were sharing was large. There was plumbing with rust-colored water. The musty bedspread was blotched and stained. The drapes were shredded by the hot sun. No television. No stopper in the bathtub. No bottled water. No radio. But no visible rats or roaches, either. Lenny looked out of the window and saw the muddy Rangoon River about a block away. Lenny and Rebecca had gotten the scenic side. The room might be livable.

Lenny and Rebecca were at the old world dining room five minutes early. Several minutes later Dana, Janet, and another gentleman — Dana's partner — arrived. Dana sat down beside Lenny, which pleased him. She had changed clothes. She was stylishly dressed, hair perfectly coiffed and wearing pearl earrings. Only the black leather money belt around her waist was incongruous, but Lenny knew the money belt was a necessity in some foreign countries. He wore a thin money holder, attached around his neck, which lay under his shirt on his chest. He still had 10 fifty-dollar bills there.

"Hi, Lenny. Hello, Rebecca. How is your room?" Dana asked.

Rebecca said, "No T.V."

Lenny quickly added, "You can tell that this was a grand old hotel when the British were here. Our room is spacious. Tell me more about your cash flow problem."

"You're not going to bill me, are you?"

"No," Lenny chuckled, "but you know the value of free advice? Really, tell me about your inventory."

"Well, I sell colored stones and some jade. As I said earlier, I bought the place last summer. I should be making a nice profit. High mark-up on my stones, but there seems to be no cash at the end of the month."

"You may have sludge in your inventory," Lenny interjected. "Have you been reducing your inventory? How often does your inventory turn over?"

Dana smiled and said, "What kind of stone is a sludge? We don't sell them. And yes, Janet and I have been trying to reduce our inventory. That is a good strategy, isn't it?"

"Reducing inventory levels can be good medicine for a company as long as sales grow and prices don't fall."

Lenny stopped as if he was turning the page of his lecture notes, then he said, "Think of your inventory of stones as a pond with an incoming and outgoing stream. But the pond has three layers of water. The top layer of water, or your inventory, is fresh water because it stays in the pond only a short period of time."

At that moment Rebecca interrupted, "Be careful, Dana, Daddy always talks shop, and he repeats things twice like he's lecturing to some undergraduate students." Rebecca laughed and turned back to Dana's partner, Frank Harrison, who was talking to Janet.

Lenny blushed slightly but continued, "This first level turns over quickly with resulting stockouts and poor service. A stockout occurs when your customer cannot find a stone she likes in your inventory. In other words, lowering service level drives off customers.

"Now the middle level of water in the pond moves more slowly because it is away from the main flow. But some of it is pulled out with the fresh water. The real problem is the third level — the sediment at the bottom of the pond. It's the sludge inventory. It may not move at all, sitting there for years. You have high holding costs which creates no value to your company." Lenny paused and then seeing Dana's evident interest, continued.

"The key is to reduce your inventory at the bottom of the pond. Decrease the amount of sludge. I have seen companies where sludge represents one-half of the inventory value, but accounts for only about ten percent of the sales. Remember, after carrying charges are deducted, these sediment sales produce no profit at all."

Lenny noticed that while he had eaten nothing from his plate, everyone else at the long table was almost finished. He began to eat the beef curry rapidly.

Dana reached over, put her hand on Lenny's arm, and said softly, "You must really enjoy your field! I could learn a lot from you, I think. We should spend some time together."

Lenny had already noticed the gold band and large pear-shaped diamond ring on her finger. "Are you married?" Lenny asked, wanting to hear that she was not, that the rings were family keepsakes.

She said, "No. I was married to Jimmy Friedman, who is executive vice-president for product design at Ascentic in Philly. We didn't get married until after I got my marketing MBA from L.S.U."

Lenny plunged ahead with the questioning. He did want to know more about her. "Where did you get your undergraduate degree?"

"Pfeiffer College. That's in North Carolina. I grew up in Somers Point, New Jersey. We have no children. You can't have a successful career and a family. I guess you make choices and you give up things. We managed to have two careers."

The waiter took Lenny's plate and he asked the group if they wanted vanilla ice cream. Rebecca's hand shot up, but Lenny raised his eyebrows and shook his head no. Rebecca frowned.

Lenny turned back to Dana and said, "What did you do before you bought your colored stone shop?"

"I was Vice-president of Consulting & Information Systems with HiTech Equipment in Boston, Massachusetts. I was HTE's first female corporate vice-president. I spearheaded our company's entry into consulting — a new line of business."

"Why did you leave HiTech?" Lenny asked.

"Oh, a number of reasons," replied Dana. "Ego mostly. The eldest son of the founder and president of the company was pushed over me. Ray Wong is bright and talented, but he has been arrogant and naive on the way up the corporate ladder. Three years ago the company had profits of $11 million, but last year it had a loss of $15 million. The company is stumbling."

"Would Wong have the top position if he wasn't related to the founder?"

"Unlikely. Besides, the company faces an uphill battle in the marketplace. I believe a woman can go far if she's dedicated and serious, but she has to try harder than men.

"My assumption at HiTech," Dana continued, "was that being a woman would not prevent me from becoming a chief executive. I did not consider someone inheriting the job. That's life. He'll spend the next 20 years of his business career being compared unfavorably to his father." Dana frowned and said, "That's enough about me. What about you?"

At that moment a waiter entered with eleven cups of ice cream and set a cup in front of each tour member. It looked good. Rebecca and Dana started eating theirs. Lenny nibbled at his ice cream. "What would you like to know about me? I like accounting. I like teaching. Consulting." Lenny took another bite of the ice cream.

"What are your hobbies?"

"Probably work."

"That figures. Besides work, what do you like to do?"

"Oh, I collected stamps as a kid. I like to play tennis. I like roller coasters. One day I would like to sky dive."

"Really? That's too dangerous for me. Do you golf?" Dana queried.

"Not much. I've tried several times." Without pausing Lenny asked, "What colored stones do you like the best? You have a beautiful diamond there." Lenny pointed to her left hand.

"Yes, that's a 2.3 carat, pear-shaped stone. My ex-husband gave it to me about six years ago. But I really like rubies too."

That night Lenny and Rebecca covered their bodies with mosquito repellent. Lenny dreamed about being inside a pear-shaped ruby prison.

* * *

The first stop Monday morning by the tour bus was outside a large building covered with sheet metal. There was a slight rain falling on a brownish sign outside the main entrance to the building:

NOTICE TO ALL TOURISTS

> Tourists are kindly requested to observe the following rules regarding mode of dress in the precincts of pagodas as prescribed by the board of trustees of the pagodas.

1. All foot wear (including socks) are strictly prohibited.
2. Shorts should not be worn. Men should wear shirts over their underwears/vests. Women should have brassieres when wearing T-shirts and blouses.
3. The pagodas are places of worship and meditation and scantly attires are considered as irreverence in Burma.

Disregard of these rules are considered as religious irreverence in Burma.

Thank you for your co-operation
Tourist Burma

Ted, the medical doctor traveling on the tour, wrapped a towel around his short pants and walked on into the building. Since most Burmese men wore plaid skirts — called longyis — rather than pants, only his white skin and camera would distinguish him from a local native — so he said. One tour member stayed on the bus rather than walk in the mud without shoes.

Lenny took his shoes off, and red mud squeezed through his toes as he walked about 20 feet through the parking lot. Inside was an unbelievable sight to an American. There was a gigantic reclining Buddha image. Called the Reclining Golden Buddha or Shwethalyaung, this impressive structure is both Burma's most beautiful and largest reclining Buddha.

The enormous face of the Buddha was propped up on his right arm staring at Lenny and Rebecca as they entered the Chauk Htat Gyi monastery. The Buddha was stretched out 216 feet to the right, surrounded by a four-foot spiked metal fence. It was impossible for Lenny to get the entire Buddha focused in his Pentax camera. It had been cut from a massive piece of marble. The robe on the Buddha was gold, trimmed in silver.

The feet at the other end appeared to be at least 30 feet tall. The bottom of the toes had red swirls like fingerprints, and there were hundreds of reddish designs carved into the bottom of the feet. Fish, tigers, cups, and other religious symbols had been carved in the hard marble. Finally Lenny climbed about 10 feet up a light pole, turned the camera sideways and got a shot of most of the Buddha.

Rebecca shouted, "Be careful, Dad." Two monks dressed in red robes walked by as Lenny was climbing down. They merely grinned; Lenny imagined that they were thinking "dumb tourist."

Back on the bus Lenny read the description on his worn itinerary about the next stop, the Shwedagon Pagoda:

> The most spectacular attraction in Rangoon contains 13,153 foot-square plates of gold, 5,451 diamonds weighing 2,078 carats, and 1,383 of rubies, sapphires, and topaz. This vast collection of riches decorates the Shwedagon Pagoda. The topmost vane with its flag turns with the wind, and the very top of the jeweled vane is tipped with a single 76-carat diamond. This pagoda, the spiritual center of Burma, attracts monks, school children, and a steady flow of Buddhist worshipers from all over Asia to its many chapels, satellite pagodas and image houses.

The Shwedagon Pagoda is not in the center of Rangoon but is three kilometers to the north. Yet to Lenny it dominated Rangoon. It rose 326 feet above its base. As they approached it in the heat of the morning, the pagoda glittered bright gold.

Rather than taking the southern stairway, the tour group took an elevator to reach the hilltop platform. Again no shoes or socks were allowed. Not only was there an admission fee, but there was a 5 kyat [say 'chat'] camera fee. Lenny paid the camera fee (which was about 70 cents in U.S. money) in order to be permitted to carry his camera inside. Lenny thought to himself, "Just another way to tax foreign tourists since the average Burmese tourists do not have cameras."

After exiting the semi-gloom of the elevator, Lenny saw

that the mighty pagoda was only one of many structures on the hilltop platform. Many of the structures were large, colorful, and beautiful — a cacophony of technicolored glitter.

Lenny touched Rebecca on the shoulder and said, "This is the Disneyland of Burma," as he surveyed the beauty with pleasure.

Rebecca turned and said, "Okay, Daddy, where are the rides? But it is beautiful. Like the colorful mountains in Bryce Canyon in Utah."

Dana touched Lenny on the back and said, "I agree. That's an astute observation. Which way are you going to walk?"

"Why not go left? That's the direction to take at all Buddhist monuments. Clockwise. We'll have to walk on that bamboo runner. This marble is hot. Can you imagine how many lives have ended trying to take and defend this magnificent hilltop?" Lenny noticed that Dana's partner was taking many photos of the area around the pagoda.

There was a wide inlaid marble-slab walkway around the Shwedagon pagoda. On both sides of the walkway were hundreds of other buildings, monuments, temples, religious symbols, bells, and pagodas. Their splashy colors sparkled in the sunlight.

"Lenny, do you know the legend behind this pagoda?" asked Dana.

"Not really," Lenny replied.

"Apparently two Mon merchants from Lower Burma obtained from the original Buddha some hair relics and on their return to Rangoon — well, it was called Dagon then. Dagon was changed to Rangoon in 1755. On their return they enshrined the hair in a small temple, which later became the kernel over which this large pagoda was built."

"How do you know this?" Lenny looked quizzically at Dana.

"I read it in one of my books last night. Janet and I couldn't sleep, so we read. By the way, Rangoon means the end of strife."

After a short pause, Dana continued, "Do you believe there's a 76-carat diamond on the top of the pagoda?" Dana pointed to the massive structure in the middle of the hilltop. Lenny looked intrigued. "You know, I thought about that too. It's hard to believe a military-backed regime would allow it to remain up there — if it was ever there. I read that the pagoda is covered with more gold than is in the Bank of England."

"There is also a very large emerald up there," Dana responded. "It catches the first rays of sun in the morning and the last rays at sundown." After a long pause she leaned closer to Lenny and asked quietly, "Some time today, would it be possible for you to touch me?"

Lenny was stunned. "But — I'm with my daughter."

"I realize I'm being forward," Dana said haltingly, "but being with you has made me smile. I've touched you several times. Consider me your friend. I like you."

She then turned and strolled down the walkway. Lenny thought she might be blushing. He knew he was.

Lenny felt rattled for some time as he walked around the pagoda.

Rather than taking the elevator, Lenny, Rebecca, Dana, and Janet walked down the long southern steps. There were many small shops waiting for tourists along both sides of the steep rock stairs.

Near the bottom of the stairs Lenny said to no one in particular, "We are walking down the same steps that Kipling climbed when he fell deeply and irreversibly in love with a Burmese girl."

Lenny managed to stand behind Dana as they boarded the bus. Gently he brushed his thumb down Dana's back. She hesitated slightly as she stepped up, but said nothing. She was smiling.

* * *

Over the next two days Lenny's morose and distracted attitude seemed to disappear, almost in proportion to his contact with Dana. She would listen entranced to Lenny, and seemed to be sincerely interested in his professional work. She entertained him with stories, too. A fleeting smile came to his face more often. By unspoken agreement, they did not discuss their prior marriages. For these few days, they were just two people in a strange country getting to know one another. On two other occasions in Rangoon, Lenny brushed against Dana in some gentle and discreet way.

From Rangoon the tour group flew to Pagan. In the terminal hundreds of birds were chattering from the rafters. Around Pagan, in the scorched wasteland was the most amazing sight to Lenny. As far as the eye could see stood over 5,000 pagodas, temples, and shrines dating back to the 11th century. Many were decaying. The evening boat ride down the Irrawaddy was even more indicative of the backwardness of Burma. Yes, middle ages was an accurate description.

Lenny saw the ox carts, carrying large drums, come down to the river to obtain the household water for the next day. Fishermen were preparing for their all-night search for food. The entire primitive social and economic structure evolved around the river. About three-quarters of the population was concentrated in the Irrawaddy basin in the south.

Mounds of dirt on the bank of the river were there to be sifted for gold and silver. Any found gold was placed on a pagoda for merits. The more merits obtained during life, the better the next life of the giver after rebirth. For centuries the Burmese have been filled with a passion for covering the country with pagodas. Building a pagoda outweighs any wrongful acts a person might do during life.

While the tour group was visiting the Shwezigon Pagoda, Dana approached Lenny and asked, "Have you exchanged any money?"

"Some at the hotels," Lenny responded.

"Have you exchanged any on the black market? The rate of exchange is much better," Dana observed.

"No, I'm afraid. It's a violation of Burmese law to exchange currency at an unauthorized place."

"Well, that guy over there has exchanged money for several of us." She gently turned Lenny around and pointed to a Burmese stranger giving something to Ted. "He's giving 25 to 1."

Lenny walked over to the man, and after darting glances from side to side, he asked, "Will you exchange money?"

"What kind?"

"U.S. dollars," Lenny said softly.

"How much?"

"$20. But can we go behind that wall?" Lenny pointed to his right.

Lenny walked cautiously behind the wall, looked around, and handed the young guy a $20 bill.

The Burmese fellow gave Lenny four stacks of bills. Lenny turned and walked rapidly back to the tour bus. Inside the bus he counted his treasury. He had only gotten 20 to 1.

Lenny rationalized, "That's much better than 7 to 1. I made a 200% return on my investment in 30 seconds." Success can quiet fear and conscience.

Lenny had read that illegal commerce was widespread throughout Burma. The domestic black market was the main source of consumer goods. In other words, a Burmese citizen could obtain better quality consumer goods from Thailand through the black market. Of course, the citizen had to have a "hard currency" such as U.S. dollars or Japanese yen in order to purchase the goods.

"I wonder if this 200% gain is taxable?" Lenny laughed to himself. "If I were a businessperson, how would I treat it on financial statements?" Of course, illegal or gambling income is taxable.

The tour bus left Pagan at five in the morning to avoid the afternoon heat. Along the narrow road to Mandalay, the small tour bus would head for the left dirt shoulder when it passed another truck. Once at a stop along the road and again at the half-way house at Meiktila, Dana came up behind Lenny and lightly ran her index finger down his back. Both times cold chills ran through his body.

After the bus left the half-way house, Ted asked, "Does

anyone know the words to the song 'On the Road to Mandalay'?" No one could think of the words.

Lenny interjected, "My father talked about the fierce fighting here during World War II. It raged to the end of the war, and Burma suffered enormous losses and major damages."

After a short pause Lenny turned to Dana and asked in a quieter voice, "What type of partnership do you have?"

"Oh, it's a limited one. I'm the general partner. Frank is the only limited partner."

"I noticed in the *Asian Wall Street Journal* last week that limited partnership sales continue to be strong," Lenny observed. He did not mention that a partnership is an association of two or more persons to carry on as co-owners of a business for a profit.

After shifting his weight in his bus seat, Lenny continued, "Does Frank take part in the control of the business?"

"Sure. He is quite helpful and I rely on his advice heavily. Why do you ask?"

"Well," Lenny answered uneasily, "if a limited partner takes part in the control of the business, then he's a general partner."

"That's interesting." Dana rolled her eyes and asked, "Would you like to know the precise date of your death?"

With a perplexed expression Lenny could only say "Eh, uh, what?"

Dana laughed out loud and then replied, "Oh, that's question number 140 in this book that I'm reading. See!" She handed Lenny a white book.

Lenny read the title: *The Book of Questions*, Gregory Stock, Ph.D.

Then Dana continued, "Why don't we answer these questions? You have to tell the truth."

For the remainder of the bus ride, Dana, Lenny, Joan Kelley, and Prawit alternately answered many personal questions from the book as the scenery sped by.

Their evening in dusty Mandalay was uneventful, and Lenny's room at the Mandalay Hotel was marginal. The air conditioner dropped the temperature somewhat, and he saw no roaches or mice. The hotel was across the street from the Royal Palace, which was totally devastated by the heavy fighting in World War II. All around were bamboo homes, ox carts, horse carriages, and dirt streets.

Up the Mandalay Hill the tour group went the next morning. The barefoot pilgrimage up the 1,700 cool, stone steps was strenuous. Lenny passed local merchants, beggars, school children, small temples, statues, and benches on the way to the top. The view at the top was worth the climb. The gigantic lions at the bottom of the hill did not look as large from the top. Also, Lenny rested his hand on Dana twice while they were looking into the devastated Royal Palace. She had told him in one of their many conversations that she had come to need this contact with him, that he quieted her as well as made her feel alive. But that was the extent of the physical contact between them. Each felt unspoken constraints.

A twin-turboprop plane with no toilet brought Lenny, Rebecca, and the tour group back to Rangoon and the Inya Lake Hotel. Lenny read the *Working People's Daily,* one of the two English newspapers, on the short flight. He mentioned to no one that he remembered that two of Burma's three aircraft had crashed within four months in 1987. One Fokker Friendship 27 crashed southeast of Pagan, and the other one crashed near their intermediate stop today — Heho. Lenny noticed the 8,200-foot-high mountain after their takeoff from Heho. The first crash had been into that mountain about 280 miles northeast of Rangoon.

After arriving safely in Rangoon, five members of the tour group went with Prawit to the Bogyoke Market. There were approximately 100 small shops at this market, and Lenny bought some lacquerware for Rebecca. In order to pay for the merchandise with U.S. dollars, Lenny had to sneak the bills to the merchant. It was illegal for the merchants in the market to accept hard currency. However, they wanted it.

Lenny spotted a finely carved old ivory Burmese dancer. The dancer was in costume, sitting in the lotus position. The piece was about five inches long and three inches wide. The first time he asked how much the merchant said "2,500 kyats." Lenny knew that old ivory costs more than a new ivory carving. This phenomenon was the reverse of most merchandizing situations. Generally, the older the inventory, the lower its price.

"How much in U.S. dollars?" Lenny asked politely.

"$100."

Lenny mentally calculated that the merchant was giving him 25 kyats per dollar. If he exchanged money at the official rate, the cost of the ivory carving would be about $357. Lenny turned and left the stall.

He returned shortly and found Dana negotiating hard with the same merchant for some jade necklaces and bracelets. The merchant was sitting in the lotus position on a raised platform surrounded by his merchandise. Prawit seemed to be helping. Dana's negotiation lasted over an hour.

At one point Lenny broke into the conversation and asked the merchant, "What is your lowest price for that ivory carving? How do I know it's real?"

"We can light a match to it. Plastic will melt. Ivory will not. This is old ivory. Very expensive. I'll let you have it for $90." Lenny got Dana's attention and asked her to get him a good price for the carving. She told the merchant, "He'll give you $40."

The merchant acted offended and said, "No! No! Too little."

Dana continued to bargain for the jade. She was trying to trade cash, Kodak film, lipstick, a pocket calculator, and other miscellaneous stuff for the jade.

During a lull in the bargaining, Prawit spoke to Dana. "Do you know that the Burmese government holds an annual Jade Emporium at Inya Lake Hotel in February? In 1983 they had a 36-ton jade boulder for sale. No one bought it, however." Dana only frowned in response.

Somehow an agreement was reached, and the merchant gave Dana the jade items. Lenny did not see Dana give the merchant any cash.

Prawit then pleaded, "We have to go now."

Dana spoke loudly to the merchant. "The carving is not worth $50. He'll give you $40. Besides, isn't ivory an endangered species? Can he get it through U.S. customs?"

"No problem. No problem. He can hide it in a sock inside a shoe in his suitcase." The merchant raised his arms as if to demonstrate that all was well.

Prawit quickly cut in, "Lenny, we have to go now."

Lenny turned to the merchant, smiled, and said, "I'll give you $50."

Shaking his head with a pained expression, the merchant shot back, "No."

Lenny turned to go. Dana picked up her packages, and Prawit began to walk away.

"Okay. $50." The merchant almost shouted.

Lenny was surprised. He had read in one of his books that you received a merchant's lowest price as you went out his door. After a pause Lenny asked the merchant, "Is a $50 bill okay?"

The merchant leaned over and handed the wrapped ivory carving to Lenny. He whispered, "Give the $50 to Prawit when you get on the plane. He'll get it back to me."

During the taxi ride back to their hotel Lenny wondered how much commission would be paid to Prawit from the transaction. Had he paid too much? Then he began to worry about customs. He had filled out a Burmese customs document declaring all of his money when he entered Burma. He had officially converted only $20 to Burmese currency. Yet he had spent well over $100. Would they lock him up for a currency violation?

His fear about rotting in prison disappeared that evening — at least temporarily. Joan Kelley had arranged for some of the tour group to visit and meet the Deputy Chief of Mission, Robert P. Samson.

Two large Chevrolets picked the group up at 8:00 at the front of the Inya Lake Hotel and drove for about 35 minutes across Rangoon to the Embassy Compound. Lenny noticed that Dana had a long conversation with Rebecca as their fancy car sped by beggars and poverty.

The Deputy Chief's house was large and modern. He indicated that it had been built with elephants for a major trading company a number of years ago.

After the normal pleasantries, Mr. Samson cocked his head and said, "Let me warn you about your travel in Burma. Cholera, hepatitis, plague, rabies, typhoid fever and malaria are endemic in Burma."

Mr. Samson paused for a moment and then continued, "Several weeks ago one of our Americans got typhoid fever — probably from the ice cream at the Strand."

Jaws dropped among the tourists. That delicious vanilla ice cream they had eaten at the Strand several nights ago could be lethal.

Dana asked, "How long does it take to catch typhoid fever?"

"The incubation period is about 10 to 14 days," responded Mr. Samson.

Lenny was now truly worried. Not only could he go to prison for currency violations, but he could also die a painful death with typhoid fever. The anxiety inherent in his growing friendship with Dana paled beside these considerations.

CHAPTER 3

> A woman noticed that a particular store always had a sign on its window indicating that all merchandise was "sold below cost." She stopped at the store, and asked the merchant how he could stay in business. The merchant said, "Oh, that's no problem; we always buy below cost."
>
> — Anonymous

Lenny did *not* have a fever, rose-colored eruptions or abdominal pains the next morning. He rationalized that the yellow fever, typhoid, and cholera shots that he took before he left on the trip would protect him. He reminded himself to be sure to take his two malaria tablets on Saturday.

He had other worries. Customs. Not only had he underestimated the amount of U.S. dollars he had when he entered Burma, but he had also spent well over $150 while in Burma. He had signed an official currency declaration when he entered Burma, and had officially converted only $20 into kyats.

Lenny was standing in front of the mirror in the upstairs bathroom at the Mingaladon airport in Rangoon. He checked the front pocket on his yellow "Hong Kong Yacht Club" shirt. The alka-seltzer cold tablets foil package looked casual to him. He touched the package, and he could feel the ivory carving inside the foil. Would the custom's officer ask to see the package?

Prawit had said earlier, "If he asks to see the carving, place these two packs of cigarettes on the counter along with the carving. Hopefully the officer will keep the cigarettes, and let you keep the ivory carving." Prawit did not suggest any other alternatives.

Lenny's hazel eyes stared back at him through the photo-tinted grey glasses as he combed his short, brown hair. There were some grey hairs, but he was not yet losing his hair. The foul odor in the bathroom brought him back from his day-dreaming, so Lenny walked downstairs just in time to move his baggage into the international flights area.

While waiting for their inspection, Lenny noticed that the customs agents were checking the luggage of some other tourist very closely. Perspiration appeared on Lenny's forehead. He tried to joke with Rebecca.

Joan Kelley came over and stopped in front of Lenny. "Can't you afford to buy shoelaces for your daughter?" She pointed to Rebecca's tennis shoes.

Lenny looked at Rebecca's black Keds. There were no shoelaces.

He shook his head in embarrassment and replied, "She probably has ten pairs at home."

"Really, Dad," Rebecca said, winking at Joan. Joan went off laughing.

Lenny fell silent for awhile and then Prawit approached the group and commanded, "Get in line over there." He pointed to a customs official. Lenny did not wish to be first or last. He got behind Ted, but just as they finished with Ted, Ted's wife broke in line in front of Lenny.

Then it was Lenny's turn. The official merely pretended to check Lenny's and Rebecca's hand luggage. He checked the 15 kyat departure tax stamp and waved Lenny to the door of the waiting room. Lenny smiled in self-satisfaction as he made his way into the waiting room. The Force was with him!

The flights from Rangoon to Bangkok (Thailand), to Jakarta (Indonesia) and to Denpasar (Bali) were time consuming. While waiting for luggage in order to go through customs in Bali,

Dana walked over to Lenny and asked in a low, passionate voice, "Could you arrange for us to be alone sometime in Bali? I wish you to kiss me." She smiled mischievously.

Lenny blinked in surprised reaction and could only respond, "I'll try."

The group stayed at the Bali Hyatt in Sanur, situated on 36 acres at the water's edge of the Badung Strait. Finally, a vacation spot with gleaming white beaches, tropical land, and live volcanoes. An unspoiled 90-mile-long beauty of lush green terraced fields of rice waited for the study tour group.

Ah, volcanoes. Lenny had always wanted to see a live one after frequently using them in his accounting classes. Lenny would tell his students that any losses or gains that arise from events that are both unusual in nature and infrequent in occurrence are classified as extraordinary. An extraordinary gain or loss is reported, net of its tax effect, separate from net operating income.

Lenny would always use an example of a loss resulting from a volcano eruption as being extraordinary. An exception would be if the particular volcano erupted on a routine basis. Lenny was excited to finally see his imaginary volcanoes first hand.

No tours were planned in Bali so five members of the group rented a van with driver and drove north toward Mt. Batur and the volcanic lake. Along the way they stopped at a wood carving factory, where Rebecca bought a wooden carving of a woman's head. The view of the volcanic lake and surrounding mountains was breathtaking. There was no live volcano, however. Returning southward again, the small van backtracked to Kuta Beach, a popular beach on the Southwest Coast. There, Lenny, Rebecca, Dana, and Janet swam in the Indian Ocean, collected seashells, and walked in the white sand.

That evening Lenny managed to be in the elevator alone with Dana. It was his first romantic kiss since the death of his beloved wife. Rebecca was looking at paintings by the local artists in the lobby.

The kiss was short and Lenny asked "What is happening?"

"I don't know," was Dana's response. "I am simply attracted to you. There is a great deal of tension."

"Tension?" Lenny repeated the word.

"Yes. You know that I was just recently divorced."

The elevator started to open and Lenny quickly said, "Will you call me when you get back to the States?"

"Sure," was Dana's simple response.

Several minutes later Lenny picked up Rebecca in the hotel lobby. She asked, "Dad, why is Dana always around you?"

"Oh, I believe that's just your active imagination."

"Sure, Dad," nodded Rebecca.

* * *

Early the next morning Lenny, Rebecca, and Janet left Bali on Singapore Airline for Bangkok and Tokyo, en route to Los Angeles and Philadelphia. Lenny and his ivory carving would have to face a U.S. customs agent in Los Angeles.

Dana and Frank Harrison took a noon Thai flight to Bangkok, Thailand. Dana sat with Frank in the smoking section.

"Did you hear that?" Frank asked Dana.

"Hear what?"

"As soon as the fasten seat belt sign goes off, at least one-half of the passengers unbuckle their seat belts. I hate it. There should be a stiff fine. If we have state laws requiring passengers to wear seat belts in a car going 55 miles per hour, certainly seat belts are needed in a 600-miles-per-hour bullet going through the air. If there's a sudden jerk, these people will be thrown on top of me."

Dana knew from experience that it was best to try to humor Frank when he began to get moody.

Dana pointed to her belt. "Look, mine is fastened, and you were right about joining a tour group in Burma. We were not checked by the Burmese customs agents when we left," smiled Dana.

Frank started to reach for a cigarette but changed his mind.

"Did you notice that Prawit gave the customs agents two bottles of whiskey? That's why they did not check the tour group. If we had gone into Burma alone, I can assure you that they would have searched us closely."

Frank lowered his voice and queried, "Did you buy the Buddha head?"

"No, the merchant only wanted cash. He would not accept my travelers checks." Dana shook her head in frustration. "And I had beat him down to a low price."

"Well, you know we have two customers who wish one." Then he whispered in Dana's ear, "I got one. We'll make 400% mark-up on it in the states."

"Do you think it will have a ruby inside the head?" Dana asked excitedly.

"Who knows? That's why we can sell it for $900 in Philadelphia."

Dana reached into her Gucci purse, pulled out a jade necklace, and handed it to Frank. "Now tell me about jade."

Frank took the necklace and slowly observed it, rubbing each stone with his fingers. He took his cigarette lighter and tapped it on several of the stones. Then he said, "Very good. It's jadeite. Jadeite occurs in an attractive, intense green that cannot be found in nephrite."

Frank paused and then said, "Let me back up. There are two types of jade — called jadeite and nephrite. Both are crystalline aggregates, composed of fibrous, intergrown crystals. Jade is tough. No other mineral can match the toughness of jade. Of course, that means jade is never absolutely transparent."

Handing the necklace back to Dana, Frank continued, "Feel the stones. No other stone can be appreciated in so many forms — sight, feel, and sound. You can see the beauty in these stones. Feel the beauty."

Frank turned to Dana and stated, "Ancient gemstone lore attributes many powers to various types of stones. Black jade gives strength and power. White jade quiets intestinal disorders. Green jade ensures high rank and authority."

Frank reached over and put his hand on the necklace in Dana's hand. "Green jade contains the concentrated essence of love, which it passes to the wearer."

Dana ignored the sarcasm and asked, "What powers do rubies have?"

"Many. A ruby ensures love and promotes passion." He smiled broadly. "A ruby ensures beauty and stops bleeding. A ruby aids firm friendship. A Capricorn who has ever worn a ruby will never know trouble."

"You're making that up." She looked inquisitively at Frank. "I'm a Capricorn. No wonder I love rubies."

Frank raised his right hand with three fingers pointing up, "Scouts' honor." He then said, "When is your birthday?"

"January 18."

"January 18, what?"

"I'm 29."

"Sure you are," Frank laughed. His irritable mood lifted somewhat.

For a moment Frank was distracted by the noise and people around him. He shifted in his seat and started again. "Empress Dowager of China, around the turn of the century, had twelve sets of jade bells hung in carved wooden frames eight feet high by three feet wide." He closed his eyes. "Can you imagine the sounds of those bells?"

Dana asked, "Is this imperial jade?" pointing to her necklace.

"Pretty close. Imperial jade or emerald jade is used to describe an intense emerald-green, semitransparent chrome-bearing jadeite. But many people believe a medium yellowish green of high intensity is the best jade — called apple green. Your stones are in between these two colors. The finest greens are caused by chromic oxide in the stone. It's the same stuff that's responsible for the color of emerald."

"Now what is the difference between jadeite and nephrite?"

"Jadeite is heavier and harder. Jadeite is shinier, and ranges in colors from white to black. There's green, yellow, blue, red, and lavender. Nephrite is a fibrous, waxy stone. A nephrite stone simply does not have the beauty or desirability of jadeite."

"Does most of the jadeite come from Burma?"

"About 90 percent. Some can be found in China, North America, and Japan. Wyoming has an attractive grayish-green nephrite."

"So why are we going to Chiang Mai tomorrow if jadeite comes from Burma?"

Frank laughed. "Do you really wish the entire story?" He faked a yawn, and put his right hand on Dana's knee.

"Frank, you're not going to start that again," Dana exclaimed.

"Look," Frank pleaded, removing his hand. "I thought I could sleep for awhile on the plane, we could buy a bottle of wine, and retire to my room this evening for a gemology lesson."

"Frank, read my lips! No! Can't you understand no? Is it in your vocabulary?"

With a mischievous smile Frank observed, "I saw you leading that Ivy League egghead Cramer around on a leash in Burma. I'm sure your boyfriend would like a detailed report of your adventure there."

Dana turned and faced Frank and her voice cracked, "And I'm sure the next customs agent would like a tip about the Buddha head in your suitcase."

She paused and continued. "You need to get married. Try your subtle technique on that Thai flight attendant." She pointed to the nearest one. "Smoke a cigarette, go to a movie, but get off my back. The answer is no deal. We are only business partners, not playmates."

They both sat in silence for several minutes. Then Frank pulled out the inflight Thai magazine and turned to the Thai route map. "Okay, okay. A truce. I'll be a good guy."

Dana said, "Besides, how do you know what I did? You were too absorbed in Janet. What did you two do — visit all 6,000 of the pagodas in Burma?"

"Look, partner, she's not married. And yes, I did give her

some jade. No big deal. Besides, I'm not a Buddhist priest — forbidden to touch or be touched by a woman, or to accept anything from the hand of a woman. Women were not even allowed in many of the temples we visited, remember?"

Dana sat looking straight ahead, brooding. "I'm sure you'll be able to get a massage tonight at the hotel," she stated.

Frank took out a pencil and began marking on a barf bag. Then he said, "Most of the world's jadeite comes from within an 80-mile radius around Hpakan, Burma. It is found in dikes of metamorphosed rocks — don't ask me how to spell it — in the Uru Valley." Frank drew a circle around the name Hpakan. "This town is about 200 miles north of Mandalay, near the India border."

"Why didn't we go there?"

"Too dangerous. That area is controlled by a rebel group called Kachin Independence Organization." Frank wrote down the initials KIO. "The military-socialist Burma government has never been able to gain control of this area. They are always fighting each other."

"Anyway, a mine owner obtains a KIO license and hires some miners. They either scour a stream bed or work a small quarry. With the aid of a water buffalo or oxen, they will haul out jade boulders weighing from a pound to several tons. The rough jade has an opaque skin somewhat like the shell of a nut."

Frank paused, caught his breath, and continued. "Suppose the miners find a promising boulder — normally in March, April, or May. During the rainy season the shafts fill up with water. The mine owner takes the boulder to Hpakan and sells it. Half of the proceeds go to the miners, who divide the proceeds equally. The owner keeps the other half, but he must give a five-percent tax to the KIO. They mark the stone as 'taxed.'"

Dana interrupted, "A tax paid to a group of warlords?"

"Apparently so. The boulder moves from Hpakan to a larger town, Mogaung, by bullock cart. Mogaung has been the jade trading center for two centuries.

"Oh, I forgot to tell you. Buying the raw material is like

buying a pig in a poke. It's a gamble all the way. Only a small window is cut into the skin of the boulder to reveal the surface color."

Frank leaned closer to Dana and continued. "In Mogaung the rough jade is sold secretly to major traders by the use of hand signals. Let me have your left hand."

"Come on, Frank. You'll live."

Stung by the insinuation, Frank took hold of Dana's left hand with his left hand. "Now, the seller and bidder put their hands under a piece of cloth. The bidder will say 'hundred' or 'thousand' out loud. The bidder will then stick out the appropriate number of fingers. For example, if the bidder says hundred and sticks out four fingers, he is offering $400."

Removing her hand, Dana asked, "What if she wishes to bid $600, $700, $800, or $900?"

Frank appeared perplexed. "You know, I don't know. Maybe *she* puts two hands under the cloth."

Dana laughed. "Frank, you're pulling my hand."

Frank raised his Scouts' honor sign again and said, "Truth! Anyway, from Mogaung the boulders go on a cavalcade of mules over clandestine trails through 400 miles of rugged border country controlled by various rival warlords. Its destination is Chiang Mai where five syndicates of Chinese Thais handle most of it. Hong Kong bidders come to Chiang Mai and take most of the boulders to Hong Kong where it is cut into jewelry and art objects. Remember Kowloon in Hong Kong. There are almost 500 jade shops and stalls along Canton Road and the nearby Jade Hawkers' Bazaar."

"I noticed mostly jewelry when we were on Canton Road. Where do they sell elaborate figurines?"

"Remember jade is very hard, so most jade is cut into jewelry or cabochon. Carving elaborate figurines is time-consuming and costly. Starting from a block of jade 16 inches square and 8 inches deep, it may take one-half year to cut a figurine using diamond drills." Frank illustrated the size of the block with his hands.

"By the way," Dana said, "I read that early Chinese often

buried bodies with jade objects. Often they put a piece of carved jade under the corpse's tongue. In fact, I thought most of the jade was cut in China."

"No longer," Frank said. "After World War II and the Communist revolution in China, many of the traders and carvers migrated to Hong Kong. They needed the free enterprise system."

"What will happen when the Chinese take over Hong Kong in 1997?" queried Dana.

"That's a good question. No one knows. That's why many professionals are obtaining foreign passports. There is and will continue to be a brain drain from Hong Kong."

"Do sellers ever try to pass off other types of stones as jade?"

"Sure," replied Frank. "Quartz, glass, enamel on metal, garnet, serpentine, and feldspar are only some of the substitutes for jade. There are fakes around."

"How do you grade jade?"

"You look at three factors: color, translucency, and evenness of color and texture. Color, of course, is the key factor. The best quality jade has an intense, evenly distributed pure green color and is semitransparent."

Frank thought for a moment and then continued. "Pierced jade is less valuable than unpierced."

"Why?"

"Well, generally, carving is used only to remove inferior material from the rough. In order to reduce labor costs, a jade boulder is cut into a design to fit the shape of the boulder. The cutter wishes to make as few cuts as possible. Jade is harder and tougher than diamonds."

Frank stopped and reached for a cigarette.

Dana said, "You don't need one."

"You're right," replied Frank, but he lit one anyway. He took three quick drags on the cigarette, and then he put it out.

"We have to worry more about jade being dyed to enhance its color. Hong Kong merchants can dye low-quality jade a rich green by heating it slowly to 212 degrees Fahrenheit and soaking it in chromium salts for several hours. This dye penetrates the cracks between the jade crystals and may fool an unsuspecting buyer."

"How can I detect such a dye job?" Dana asked.

"It's hard, but be careful of a green color that seems to float on the surface of the jade. Here the dye has not penetrated deeply."

Frank stopped for a moment and then asked, "Do you know about irradiation stones? Colors of stones may be enhanced by being exposed to radiation, especially celestial blue topaz from a white topaz or a milky white sapphire to a translucent blue."

"Isn't that dangerous?" asked Dana.

"Reputable U.S. firms are trustworthy since the Nuclear Regulatory Commission will not allow any gems released until they have properly cooled down. But you probably need to buy a Geiger counter and carry it with you on gem-buying trips."

"Should I avoid irradiated gems?"

"Probably only the hot ones. Irradiation has become about as acceptable to the gem industry as heat-treated stones. Now the real controversy is with crystal growers."

"You can grow gems?" Dana appeared shocked.

"Absolutely," Frank replied. "There is even a Gemstone Crystal Growth Association. Natural-gem people label laboratory-grown gem crystals as synthetic, but the crystal growers despise this term."

"What gems can be grown?" queried Dana.

"Well, obviously cultured pearls. There are Chatham-created emerald, a Ramaura ruby — I remember an ad a number of years ago. It had a box with a cereal bowl filled with created emeralds. The box said '100% natural ingredients. Chatham-created emeralds. Chatham-created emeralds, the natural man-made gemstone.' Obviously there was an outburst of protest from the natural gem people."

"Can I detect a lab-grown gem?"

"The best growers use a hydrothermal or flux method. Responsible growers will dope their products so they can be identified as lab-grown. But there are many irresponsible people. Now a lab-grown emerald is actually a purer form of emerald. They can be grown flawless. Natural emeralds are seldom flawless."

"What's the future for lab-grown gems?" Dana asked.

"It's impressive. They argue that an orchid that is grown in a hothouse is still a real orchid — so why is a lab-grown gem not a real gem? Remember, they use the same ingredients as Mother Nature."

Dana thought for a moment. "How long can it be before the Japanese start growing gems and flooding the market?"

"Good point," replied Frank. "But worry more about Thailand."

"That reminds me," Dana interjected, "we purchased a new diamond detection machine before I left on this trip. Do we expense it?"

"How much did it cost?"

"About $550."

"Will it last more than a year?"

"Sure," responded Dana. "As long as they don't invent a new kind of fake diamond."

"That's the answer. There's a matching principle in accounting. Costs of generating our revenues must be matched against the revenue in the accounting period when the revenue is earned. We match the cost of equipment by a depreciation procedure. The $550 cost will be allocated to each accounting period over the useful life of the equipment, or the period of time until the machine's physical life is exhausted," explained Frank. "Suppose the useful life is ten years. Using the straight-line method, each year for ten years we'll show $55 as a depreciation expense. In order to smooth income for financial statement purposes, we'll probably use the straight-line method."

"What about for tax purposes?"

"We'll use an accelerated method for our tax return — basically 200 percent declining balance method. In other words, more depreciation will be taken in the early years of the asset.

You can logically defend the accelerated method since maintenance probably increases as the depreciation expense decreases over the life of the asset. Thus, you are smoothing the total expenses over the asset's useful life. In fact, we can write the detection machine off over a six-year period. The higher our depreciation expense, the less taxable income, and, therefore, a smaller tax liability."

"What do we do with this difference in tax expense between financial and tax accounting?"

"Any difference between our income tax expense, which is based on our accounting income, and our income tax liability goes into an account called deferred taxes. It is treated similar to a liability." Frank smiled in self-satisfaction.

"I've had enough accounting. What's the saying? Accountants never die, they just lose their balance. Tell me about Thailand."

"Ah, Thailand, the crossroads of Southeast Asia. About the size of France, it is the only country in the Far East that was not colonized by the Europeans. Thailand is an enchanting Buddhist kingdom where the past and present mingle in perfect harmony — if you believe the travel brochures. A constitutional monarchy, but ruled silently by the military. You'll see more olive-drab military uniforms than saffron-robed monks. I like Bangkok. It's a shame we're going directly to Chiang Mai. Bangkok's Grand Palace is a spectacular building. Did you see 'Bridge on the River Kwai'?"

"Sure," said Dana.

"The 'Death Railway' was built by POWs over the Meklang River — known to the rest of the world as the River Kwai. The Thai government capitulated immediately to the Japanese invasion in World War II and the country suffered no damages. Not like the bloody jungle battles of Upper Burma. Did you know that the treacherous Burma Road is said to have cost exactly one man per mile?"

Dana shook her head and was silent for a moment. Frank then resumed.

"The official language is Thai, but they understand English in hotels, shops, and restaurants. My last trip I saw Thai-style boxing at the Lumpini Stadium. A ritual preceded each bout. There was classical Thai music and the barefooted gladiators roared around attacking each other with fists — no gloves — elbows, knees, and bare feet. The crowd jeered and shouted as they gambled in the aisles." Frank made a half-flapping gesture with his hands. "The bouts consisted of five three-minute rounds with two-minute intermissions. You cannot see such action like that in the States, except maybe at a pit bull fight."

Dana frowned and replied, "Sounds gross to me. What's the music for?"

"To give the boxers rhythm and encouragement, of course. Maybe we can see a martial art movie in Chiang Mai."

Frank sat silent for some time as if exhausted, and then he handed Dana the barf bag and the inflight magazine and began reading the *International Herald Tribune.*

Dana almost thanked him for all the information she had been given, but was wary of appearing to encourage his personal attention. Instead she opened up the magazine and began reading an article on page 36 entitled "Diversions: Bangkok 1928."

Their stay in the modern Don Muang Airport in Bangkok was short. Dana did stroll around the airport, after converting $50 into 1350 bahts. [A baht is about 3 cents in U.S. currency.] One of the paintings on the wall entitled "Swan Lake" was so lifelike that she took a photograph of it.

About 500 air miles later Dana and Frank arrived at the City of Roses. Northwest of Bangkok, Chiang Mai is the cultural capital of the north and the world's largest center of such cottage industries as silk, wood carvings, silverware, charmingly painted umbrellas, temple bells, and pottery. In this small city of about 100,000 people located in a fertile valley, a person can bicycle around its old moat in 30 minutes. A short taxi ride and 150 baht took them to Chiang Mai Orchid Hotel.

After four days and nights in Burma, the Orchid Hotel was

beautiful to Dana. The decor inside was of Thai-Burmese design, and there were lovely woods, carvings, and weavings throughout the hotel. Dana was so exhausted she fell asleep early.

Dana met Frank at 7:30 the next morning in the three-tiered Mae Rim coffee shop. Cimi Kiengsiri, their dark-skinned local guide and a student at Chiang Mai University, was already eating when Dana arrived. After a hearty breakfast, Frank, Dana, and Cimi walked to a four-wheel-drive Nissan for their trek to the hilltribe region near where Thailand, Burma, and Laos touch. Known as the Golden Triangle, the area is the smuggling capital of the Far East — especially for opium.

They took Route No. 108 from the town for about 35 miles and Cimi turned right on a byroad for 5 miles. There in front of them was the Mae Klang Waterfall. Cimi spoke reasonable English. "The Mae Klang Waterfall is the best known waterfall in Thailand and it rushes down from a height of 99.4 feet."

Before leaving the waterfall Cimi took a rifle and shotgun from his trunk. Dana knew that the trip today to Mae Sai could be extremely dangerous. Back on Route No. 108 Cimi pointed out the entrance road to Doi Inthanow, a national park with Thailand's highest mountain. After about two more hours of driving past many temperate fruit fields and elephants working in the teak forest, Cimi parked the Nissan when the dirt road literally stopped, and they began their hike through an area barely touched by the twentieth century. Through teak forests and thick jungles, past mist-shrouded mountain scenery, the three traveled for three hours in order to reach a native village called Mae Sai. They were in the lower extremes of the Himalayan foothills. The greatly increased humidity kept them from enjoying the slightly decreased heat.

The village was composed mostly of huts. At the north end of the village they met a group of men dressed in floppy hats, bush shirts, jeans, and sneakers. They were carrying shotguns and rifles and seemed to be guarding about twenty mules. The mules were carrying pack saddles to which heavy sacks were roped.

Frank spoke to Cimi and pointed to one of the mules. "Take Dana over there and show her some raw materials. I need to talk to the boss of this group." Frank walked over and began talking to a brute of a man.

From the corner of her eye, Dana saw a large rat race from beneath one of the small huts toward the underbrush. Right behind the rat was a pale brown snake about three feet long. One of the guards sitting under a tree jumped up and shot at the snake with both barrels of his shotgun. He missed.

Dana turned to Cimi and asked, "Why did he do a foolish thing like that? He could have shot someone!"

Cimi had seen the snake also. He smiled and replied, "That was a Russell's Viper. They are more deadly than a cobra."

"A Russell's Viper?" Dana repeated. "I've never heard of such a snake."

"Well, kid, if that snake bites you, death would occur within minutes. About the only way to survive is to have a doctor with you. That snake can kill an elephant."

"It was a pretty snake," Dana interjected. "There were three rows of large black rings along the body of the snake. If they are so deadly, why don't they eliminate them?"

"Too many rodents around for them to eat. The bad human conditions and the warm climate are conducive to a large snake population. One mother snake can have a litter of about two dozen babies," offered Cimi.

Cimi directed Dana to one of the mules and he spoke in Burmese to one of the men. The man got up from his resting place under a large teak tree. He opened one of the sacks, pointed inside, and said, "Chous Seine. Jade."

Dana saw a brown rock about the size of a basketball. She said to Cimi, "Ask him if I can see the window."

Apparently the tribesman understood English because he took the boulder out, placed it on the ground, and pointed to a small cut in the shell-like rock.

Dana could see the green surface color. She asked the tribesman, "Is this a good piece of jade? Does the green color go throughout the rock?"

The tribesman took an old beat-up flashlight from his knapsack and shined it into the cut. He said, "Good color. Good stone. Very valuable."

Cimi laughed and said, "Pure gamble."

From the corner of her eye Dana saw Frank give a large manila envelope to the caravan leader. They shook hands and smiled, and then Frank went over to the mule.

"So how is the raw material? They'll sell this load to one of the Thai Chinese bosses in Chiang Mai. Most of it will go to Hong Kong. Have you seen enough?"

Sweat was running down Dana's back and face. Her blouse felt soaked from perspiration. "You bet," was her only reply, as she wiped her right hand over her forehead and threw her sweat on the ground. Early March to the end of May was the hot season.

Back on the trail Dana approached Frank and asked, "Who were those men?"

"They're Shan tribesmen. They just brought the jade across the border from Burma. They're probably members of the Kachin Organization. Tough characters," Frank answered.

Dana then asked, "What did you give him in the manila envelope?"

"Oh, a small bribe, my address, and some other information about myself. Also, a letter from Fred Brown, one of our suppliers. I hope to establish a source for jade rocks."

Frank immediately changed the subject "What did Profes sor Cramer tell you about our cash flow problem?" he asked as he slapped a mosquito from his arm.

"He was talking about inventory sludge. I really don't know. What inventory method do we use?"

"We use specific identification. Most jewelers do. Costs are assigned to cost of goods sold and ending inventory by identifying a specific cost incurred with *each* unit sold and *each* unit in ending inventory. For example, if a specific jade carving remains in inventory at the end of the year, the cost of that carving is included in ending inventory. This actual cost flow method is quite appropriate for us because we have a small volume of separately identifiable units in our inventory. Since we use the specific identification system, we also combine it with the perpetual system. In other words, the cost of each gem or carving is identified as it is sold."

"What happens if a jade carving is stolen by a customer?" At that moment a limb on a tree flew back and hit Dana in the mouth. She could taste blood in her mouth, and she took out a handkerchief to press it against the inside of her lip.

"Our perpetual inventory system will give us an ending inventory figure at the end of the year. This figure is then compared with our physical inventory count at year end. The difference is our inventory shrinkage — theft, breakage, and so forth. It's an expense of doing business."

"Maybe I should take an accounting course," Dana said almost to herself.

"No need," replied Frank. "You have Janet and me. You should probably take the Gemological Institute of America's Colored Stone Course."

By sunset Frank, Dana and Cimi reached their parked car. Frank asked Dana, "Do you still wish to go to the ruby mines along the border of Cambodia — it's called Kampuchea now. It's south of Bangkok and dangerous."

"No, thank you. I've had enough of walking. Is there anything else we can do in Bangkok?"

Frank smiled, hesitated, and then decided to forgo a snide remark. Dana noticed the hesitation and silently congratulated Frank on wisely deciding against an irritating remark.

Frank finally replied, "I could get us into a Thai laboratory which cooks gemstones. They specialize in rubies and sapphires."

"I would like that," Dana replied.

On the trip back to Chiang Mai, Frank began drawing on a sheet of paper and then handed it to Dana in the back seat. "Here's a diagram of our inventory process. You'll have to use this flashlight."

Dana reviewed the penciled outline with the help of a flashlight:

Cost of beginning jade inventory + Cost of purchase	=	Cost of jade available for sale	=	Cost of ending jade inventory	→ Balance sheet
				+	
				Cost of jade sold + Shrinkage	→ Income statement

She then said, "Not bad. I can understand that."

At 2:30 the next evening Frank and Dana arrived at Corelab, a high security gem treatment laboratory. Only 20 minutes from Bangkok's downtown jewelry district, the cybernetically controlled laboratory is hidden by shrubbery and patrolled by guard dogs. Inside Frank introduced Dana to Ken Ho, the computer genius of the ten computer-controlled electric ovens.

Mr. Ho pointed to one of the ovens. "A computer controls the temperature of the ovens by taking readings of the treatment process every five seconds. No longer is the gem-burning done in an oil drum insulated with coconut rinds."

Dana asked, "What is your success rate?"

"We do pick gemstones that show promise of improvement, and we have a success rate of about 90 percent," Mr. Ho answered.

"How long do you treat rubies and sapphires?" Dana inquired.

"Each parcel of gems may be cooked for a few hours or as long as a week. It depends on what is necessary."

"What does the computer do?" Frank asked.

"The computer does what a person can do but does it 1,000 times faster. Basically the computer monitors the temperature and automatically adjusts the heat and the atmosphere to ensure that the duration and intensity of each phase of the gem-burning follows the prescribed instructions."

Mr. Ho pointed to a colored photo on the wall showing two parcels of rubies. "Notice the red rubies on the right. They've received treatment. The pinkish ones on the left were from the same lot before treatment."

"What is the charge for this treatment?" Dana asked.

"We break each parcel of stones into three lots. The client gets two lots and we take one lot for payment."

"Has the industry accepted heat treatment?" Dana inquired.

"Almost an accepted industry practice today," was Mr. Ho's response.

After bidding good-bye to Mr. Ho, Dana and Frank visited several gem factories that afternoon. Early the next morning they left for their return trip to Philadelphia.

CHAPTER 4

> As a general rule, a witness may only testify to facts and leave inferences or conclusions to the judge or jury. An expert witness, on the other hand, may testify in the form of an opinion based not only upon those facts perceived by the expert, but on facts perceived by others, as well, and made known to the expert at or before the trial; this may include the evidence or testimony of others.
>
> — Francis C. Dykeman

Lenny had hoped for a call from Dana Scott when she returned from her trip. But she did not call, so Lenny finally called her at her jade shop. They agreed on a meeting at an out-of-the-way restaurant south of the city the following evening. Lenny arrived early at the Fishhouse and ordered a diet Coke. Five minutes later Dana sat down at his table.

"Hello, good looking!" a cheerful voice said. "How was your day?"

"Average. Would you like a lite beer?"

"Sure would."

"How about your day?" Lenny asked casually.

"This afternoon was different. We apparently had a professional gem switcher in the shop today."

"What happened?" Lenny asked.

"Janet, our bookkeeper, was helping out this afternoon. We were busy. She was showing a two-carat ruby to a male customer. Apparently he was a switch artist. Anyway, Janet was distracted, and he ripped us off."

"How did it happen?" Lenny was more interested now.

"Oh, these guys use cigarettes or glasses as props. They get a lot of movement going with their hands, and zap! They switch the stone. He switched it with a garnet. Now we use locking tweezers, but he apparently had cased the store before. He asked Janet to see a particular two-carat ruby, and then switched both the ruby and the tweezer. He's smooth."

"What did you do?"

"I called around and apparently this same guy has hit about six people on the street. One jeweler told me that this fellow hit him twice. He vaguely recognized him from an earlier theft. He swore to me that he never took his eyes off of the guy, yet he made the switch. He got a second diamond from him and left a CZ."

"What's a CZ?"

"Cubic zirconia. Looks like a diamond but weighs about twice as much."

Abruptly Dana changed the subject. "I really need to hire you. My cash flow problem is not any better. I worry that either Frank or Janet may be taking money from my business — somehow. A sleuth like you should be able to solve the mystery."

"Maybe you're just not playing the float game well enough," Lenny suggested.

"Does that have to do with inventory?" She laughed out loud.

"Not completely," replied Lenny. "You need to shorten the elapsed time between the sale of your gems and the actual time the monies are collected and deposited into your bank account. This involves your method of billing and your method of bill delivery. There are a whole range of cash management devices."

"For example, Lenny?"

"Suppose you get a purchase order. The invoice should be prepared from the purchase order and mailed immediately. It doesn't matter if the invoice reaches the customer before the merchandise does. The customer will put the bill into a current payment file and you'll get paid ahead of other people."

"I'm not sure such a change would make a significant difference in my shop," Dana protested.

"Well, I need to spend some time at your jade shop."

A disinterested waiter brought the beer, and as he left, Dana smiled and said, "I'm interested in your proposition that we spend some time together."

"Great. You have made my day. Why are you interested?"

"Oh, probably because of your pleasant personality and sense of humor."

Lenny spent an enjoyable hour talking with Dana. When they parted, Lenny promised to call her in several days. Too bad, Lenny thought. "I wish I didn't have to prepare for my day in court tomorrow."

* * *

"Professor Cramer, for the court's record, please state your full name and current address."

"Paul Leonard Cramer, the third, 1245 Liberty Court, Philadelphia, Pennsylvania."

"Dr. Cramer, we wish to thank you for testifying today as an expert witness about certain accounting matters. First, I have several questions for you concerning your background. Where did you obtain you Ph.D. degree?"

"University of Illinois."

"Where did you receive your MBA degree?"

"Harvard University."

"Where did you receive your bachelor's degree?"

"Amherst."

"Are you listed in Who's Who in America?"

"Yes."

"What years were you president of the American Accounting Association?"

"That was 1989–90."

Lenny had rehearsed most of these questions and answers

before. Lenny liked the grueling task of preparing beforehand and participating in a courtroom battle over accounting principles. There was the challenge to react and respond to the many trick questions asked by the opposing attorney. Probably the stress was not worth the daily fees he received, but he loved it. He sometimes imagined the opposing attorney to be a black-clad medieval knight racing toward him on horseback with a long, sharp lance. Lenny always toppled the vicious knight in his daydreams.

"Professor Cramer, have you written any accounting books?"

"I have written four accounting books. Two principles of accounting textbooks, a forensic accounting book, plus an accounting casebook for MBA students."

"Would you please explain what is meant by forensic accounting?"

"Briefly, forensic accounting is a science that deals with the relation and application of accounting facts to business and social problems." Lenny smiled and turned toward the jury. "As I tell my students, a forensic accountant is like the Columbo or Quincy characters of yesteryear, except he uses accounting records and facts to uncover fraud, missing assets, insider tradings and other white-collar crimes." Lenny turned back to the pinstriped lawyer.

"Dr. Cramer, where are you currently employed?"

"I am the Sidney Paton Professor of Accounting, Wharton's School, University of Pennsylvania."

"Is it an honor to hold a professorship?"

"Yes, there are few professorships in accounting." Lenny thought, "Yes, no money, just a title. The real money is in a 'chair' designation." Lenny was still searching for a chair designation at an agreeable university.

"Professor Cramer, are you a Certified Public Accountant?"

"Yes, in Pennsylvania, since 1970," Lenny responded.

"Are you a member of the American Institute of CPAs?"

"Yes, since 1970."

"Do you serve on the Board of Directors of any major corporations?"

"Yes, I serve on the Board of Directors of four of the top *Fortune* one hundred companies and for three smaller companies."

"Dr. Cramer, are you an outside consultant?"

"Yes, I have my own forensic accounting firm here in Philadelphia. I started it about seven years ago."

"Please estimate how many professional articles you have written."

"About 70." Lenny shifted in the wooden chair.

"Uh." The attorney shuffled several pages and then continued, "have you ever appeared as an expert witness in the courtroom?"

"Yes. I have been an expert witness for accounting matters on about eleven different occasions — two oil companies, two banks, one insurance company, a manufacturing company, an accounting firm, the Internal Revenue Service, the SEC, and two divorce cases."

"What is the SEC?"

"Sorry." Lenny blushed slightly. "The SEC refers to the Securities and Exchange Commission. The SEC was created by the Securities Exchange Act of 1934. It has the legal authority to prescribe accounting methods for firms whose shares of stocks and bonds are sold to the investing public on the stock exchanges. The law requires that such companies make reports to the SEC, giving detailed information about their operations. The SEC regulates the amount and type of information to be included in annual and quarterly reports and the methods to be used to develop the information. For the most part, the SEC has followed the standards established by the FASB concerning the methods used to develop the required information."

"What is the FASB?" the lawyer asked.

"FASB stands for the Financial Accounting Standards Board that began to issue standards in 1973. The SEC has charged this seven-member independent nongovernmental body with the responsibility of developing and issuing standards of financial accounting affecting the private sector of the United States. Committee members include public and nonpublic accountants as well as non-accountants. In short, the FASB is our current source of Generally Accepted Accounting Principles for which accountants use the acronym GAAP."

The attorney turned to the judge and said, "Your honor, we present to this court Dr. Cramer, as an expert witness in the area of forensic accounting."

The robed judge turned to the opposing attorney and said, "Mr. Henderson, do you have any objections to this request?"

The opposing attorney stood up and spoke loudly, "No, your honor."

"So moved. You may proceed, counselor."

Lenny answered a number of technical questions that he had previously rehearsed. Then the opposing attorney began his questioning. His questions focused on the idea of the reporting of income tax expense for an oil company involved in the lawsuit.

"Now, Professor Cramer, under FASB 69 are the terms net income or net profits used?" the attorney asked.

"Not in FASB 69," responded Lenny, "although it is generally understood that results of operations are approximately equivalent to net income and net profits, and some companies in fact use the term net income and net profits in their FASB 69 disclosures."

"Those companies are the exception, rather than the rule?" Mr. Henderson asked.

"Well, I have looked at many companies, but I haven't made a comprehensive study of it, so I really can't tell you."

The attorney whispered to the assisting attorney on his right and then turned back to Lenny. "Also when you said earlier that income taxes are one of several costs in the computation of net income and net profits and are deducted along with other taxes on, or measured by, profits or income, are you saying that classification of expense items is irrelevant for accounting purposes?"

Lenny thought for a moment and then said, "Well, to paraphrase another accounting theorist, A. L. Littleton, who wrote in the nineteen-forties, all costs have equal standing as far as being recovered in the determination of income. I don't believe that any one particular cost is somehow superior to another from an accounting standpoint."

"Professor Cramer, I didn't imply any kind of qualitative superiority. I asked whether the classification of costs itself, the various items of cost under GAAP, is irrelevant."

Lenny shifted in the hard seat and replied, "Well, it depends on the circumstances. I have seen expenses lumped together. I've seen them expressed in extremely high levels of detail.

"Personally, I believe there are certain minimum standards on some items with respect to how they are disclosed, but as far as what level of detail is required, it depends on the specific situation. I mean, you have to give me a situation with a specific example."

"Perhaps," the attorney posited as he walked towards Lenny, "you should tell us what an income statement does."

"The income statement is the financial statement that measures the success of the operation of an enterprise for a distinct period of time. It provides investors, creditors, and other users with information that helps them predict the amount, timing, and uncertainty of future cash flows."

In a half-question, half-statement, the attorney then said, "And the income statement consists of revenues less expenses, does it not, Professor Cramer?"

"Yes, that is true."

The attorney cleared his throat and then asked, "Well, does FASB 96 require a separate reporting of income taxes on a separate line?"

Lenny turned to the half-listening judge and stated, "FASB 96 is concerned primarily with the difference between income tax expense as reported on the financial statements versus what's on the corporate tax return, and I would have to look at the specific provisions to see exactly what it says."

"Professor Cramer, could you explain what timing differences are?"

Lenny sighed. "Ed Deakin, a Texas professor, describes this well. 'A timing difference arises when there is a different method used for recognizing a revenue or expense for financial reporting purposes from the method used for reporting taxes. An example would be depreciation. The total amount to be depreciated is the same for both financial reporting and tax filing. The allocation of depreciation expense each year, however, will differ if the same depreciation method is not employed. The difference between the two methods is a timing difference that causes the amount of reported income tax expense to differ from the amount of income tax paid.'"

"Well," the attorney said, his voice rising, "it is true that FASB 96 does address the question of the timing differences in the reporting of income tax, but to know what taxes you have to account for, you have to know whether they are treated as an income tax under FASB 96, isn't that so?"

Lenny hesitated and then stated, "I think you're asking me to draw a conclusion about FASB 96, which at this point I'm not prepared to draw. I would like to look at FASB 96 and see what it says, and then perhaps I can help you with the interpretation."

The attorney acted offended. "Well, I believe you cited FASB 96 in your report, did you not?"

"Yes, but I don't believe I cited a provision which says you have to report income taxes on a separate line in the income statement."

At this point Lenny began to get irritated with the attorney. Lenny knew in general that FASB 96 dealt with accounting for income taxes, and he knew the general provisions, but he was not a walking encyclopedia who could quote every single word of the Opinion.

"Professor Cramer, I've had marked for identification a volume entitled Financial Accounting Standards, Original Pronouncements as of June first, 1988, and in particular, pages 187 to 202 which contains FASB 96, and I direct your attention to paragraph number sixty and ask whether you'd be able to respond to my question after examining that exhibit." The attorney walked to Lenny and handed him the open book.

After reading the marked paragraph, Lenny looked up and began speaking slowly, distinctly and firmly. He knew that everything that was said by a witness was taken down by the court reporter. "If I may, I'll restate the question for the record, since it's been a bit of time since we went through it. The question was on the order of does FASB 96 require reporting of income taxes on a separate line. In paragraph sixty it states — if I may, I'll quote it and let it stand for itself — 'In reporting the result of operations the components of income tax expense for the period should be disclosed.'

"The answer to your question is no; it does not require disclosure of income tax expense on a separate line." Lenny chuckled to himself, and thought, "The one thing about a courtroom — it's sometimes boring."

The attorney smiled. "Well, within the variations of timing differences, are income tax expenses under the income statement reported separately?"

"I have seen them reported as a line item income tax expense which includes part of the income tax expense, but not all of it. I have seen extraordinary items reported gross with the income tax subtracted from them. I have seen extraordinary items reported net of the income tax effect. I've seen income tax expense disclosed in a variety of ways, not just as a separate line item."

The attorney took a drink of water and then stated, "Professor Cramer, I understand your answer to be that income taxes *may* be reported under operations, under extraordinary items, *or* in a category of corrections on the income statement. My question to you is as follows: Are income taxes under GAAP reported on a separate line in determining income from operations?"

"Generally, there is a line item that says income tax expense that's related to the results of operations for — let's say on the financial statements."

The attorney interjected, "Including the income statement, when you refer to financial statements?"

Lenny replied, "Yes, including the income statement."

"Does FASB 96 require separate reporting of income tax expense in determining income from operations?" He looked directly at Lenny.

"Let me look at FASB 96 again." Lenny read for a moment and then explained, "FASB 96 says that the components of income tax expense should be disclosed. It says that there should be an allocation of the items, and it gives some options on how they are disclosed."

Lenny paused and then continued, "I believe Professor Sidney Davidson wrote about the depreciation problem as one of the major items of timing differences resulting from differences between what companies were reporting, the income tax that they were actually paying, when in fact they had this large contingent liability that was going to catch up with them when the timing differences were reversed."

Lenny caught his breath and then continued. "That was the focus of FASB 96, and now we're trying to convert that to a statement of whether FASB 96 requires some specialized disclosure of income tax expense itself, and it allows an option in the way in which taxes are disclosed.

"My own feeling on this, I mean a free floating sort of feeling or freebee that I'll offer for you, is that *yes,* it requires a disclosure of income tax expense as defined within FASB 96."

Lenny stopped, poured a glass of water, and took three sips. "It allows a variety of disclosures. It certainly requires some reconciliation between what has actually been reported on the income tax statement and the income as it is reported on the financial statements. To the extent that there is no material difference between the income tax expense as reported on the financial statements and the income taxes reported to the IRS, FASB 96 simply would not apply. There is no material difference, and hence, there is no problem there."

"Professor Cramer, please try to speak in laymen's language. When you refer to options available under FASB 96, aren't you really talking about the manner in which the components of the income tax expense are either disclosed on the face of the income statement or explained further in footnotes?"

Lenny knew that the attorney was trying to discredit his testimony. "If I understand your question, what you're saying is that there's got to be a disclosure of those tax expenses. When they are material, they are disclosed in the statements in some shape or form, and there is a subsequent disclosure either in the statements *or* in the notes thereto which explains what's going on with the income taxes that are covered by FASB Number 96."

Lenny paused and then continued, "But, again, if the income tax expense under FASB 96 is the same for financial reporting purposes as it is on the tax return, then a simple disclosure of the amount is sufficient, and it can be on the face of the statement or it can be someplace else in the notes."

"Professor, are you familiar with the reporting of income tax expense by oil companies — integrated oil companies — on their income statement?"

"Yes, I am," Lenny responded.

"Do you know of any oil company that reports the windfall profit tax as an income tax expense on its income statement?" the lawyer fired back.

"Typically, it's listed as windfall profit tax, which is a separate line item from the other income tax expenses," Lenny answered calmly. "Remember, the windfall profit tax was an *excise* tax — not an *income* tax."

"The answer is you're not aware of any oil company that reports windfall profit tax as an income tax expense on its income statement or financial statements?"

"That's correct," Lenny answered loudly.

A few more minor questions followed before Lenny's testimony was complete. From his previous experience as an expert witness, he had learned to restate the interrogator's question to suit his own purpose. He was pleased that things went smoothly today at the hearing.

After exchanging pleasantries with some people he had met before, Lenny quickly grabbed a cab to go back to his university office. He had to review his lecture on dividends for preferred stock. Along the way he read his semimonthly *The CPA Letter,* which was published by the American Institute of CPAs. He made a note in his calendar under September 19–23: "AICPA annual meeting, N.Y.C." He also made a note to order a free speech from the Institute entitled "How CPAs Solve the Problems of Small Business Owners." The title of the speech reminded him of Dana Scott's cash problem and the unclear status of his personal relationship with Dana.

* * *

"Lenny, you're back early."

Lenny turned around and smiled. He recognized Woody's voice right away. "My testimony ended quickly and I figured that I would come back to the office and prepare my lecture for tomorrow."

"What's the lecture on?" inquired Woody.

"Dividends for preferred stock."

"I'll give you a hand with it," Woody smiled.

Lenny was very familiar with this pattern of Woody's behavior. Woody often would hang out in Lenny's office to avoid working. Most people knew that if they needed the janitor, they should come to Lenny's office because Woody would probably be there. On more than one occasion, Lenny had come to his office and found Woody asleep in Lenny's easy chair.

"Tell me how this sounds, Woody. Preferred stock is similar to bonds payable, because both securities pay a percentage on their respective par values."

"No good," grumbled Woody as he eased back in the easy chair. "What's par value? Is it a golf score or what?"

Lenny smiled. He enjoyed going through class preparation with Woody. Lenny felt confident that if Woody could understand what he was talking about, any student could too.

"Par value does nothing more than establish the maximum responsibility of a stockholder in the event of insolvency. It is a value that is used to record the preferred stock when it is issued. It is from the par value of preferred stock that dividends are calculated."

"How's that?" Woody asked as he stuck a piece of Doublemint gum in his mouth.

"Give me a second, Woody," Lenny said laughingly. "I didn't realize that your desire for knowledge was so strong."

"Yeah, I'm that way about accounting for preferred dividends," retorted Woody with a sheepish grin.

"I'm always happy to lecture to students with a thirst for knowledge," replied Lenny, becoming more serious. "Let's see. To calculate preferred dividends, all one has to do is multiply the par value by the percentage associated with the preferred stock. For example, if there is eight percent preferred with $100 par value, all one does is multiply the eight percent by $100, and the dividends are eight dollars per preferred share. If there are one thousand shares of preferred stock outstanding, then total preferred dividends are eight thousand dollars."

"What if your stock is not outstanding — like some stock my brother-in-law bought three years ago and is now worthless?" grumbled Woody as he put his feet up on Lenny's desk. "That stock was certainly not outstanding."

"That's what your brother-in-law gets for listening to his so-called friends with good tips," said Lenny, making reference to the boasts of Woody's brother-in-law that he had friends in the mob. "Outstanding has a different meaning with respect to stock. Shares outstanding are the shares of a corporation's stock that are outside of the control of the corporation. Shares authorized are the number of shares the corporation may distribute as indicated in its corporate charter. Shares issued are the number of shares of stock distributed by the corporation."

"What's the difference between the number of shares issued and the number outstanding?"

"You're paying attention today, Woody," remarked Lenny with a grin.

"Always do," garbled Woody, as he placed an unlit cigar in his mouth.

"Once stock is originally sold, it is issued and outstanding. If the stock is repurchased as treasury stock, the stock is still issued, but no longer outstanding." Lenny paused and stared at Woody. "Are you ever going to smoke that cigar? You've been putting that same cigar in your mouth for three months without lighting it up."

"It's healthier this way." Woody fingered the cigar, looked at it, and then stared back at Lenny. "There doesn't seem much to preferred stock dividends, does there?"

"Hold on, Woody, I haven't even mentioned what to do if the preferred stock is cumulative." Lenny took a deep breath and continued. "My previous example was based on the assumption that the preferred stock was non-cumulative. If the preferred stock is cumulative, the stockholder is guaranteed a dividend each year. Using the previous example, the preferred dividend of eight dollars per year is guaranteed. If the corporation fails to pay out dividends for one year, then the dividends are considered to be one year in arrears. That would mean that preferred stockholders would receive sixteen dollars per share the next year. If there was no cumulative feature, the preferred shareholder would only receive eight dollars per share regardless of whether dividends were in arrears. Remember that common stockholders can receive no dividends until the obligation to preferred stockholders is completely satisfied."

"I'll keep that in mind," Woody replied in the middle of a yawn. "Is that it?"

"That's it. Pretty easy, huh?" asked Lenny, eyebrows raising.

"Not bad." Woody leaned forward in his chair. "I had a big winner at the racetrack the other day. It paid 8 to 1."

"What was its name?"

"Dana's Revenge."

Dana. Lenny wondered how she was doing. It had been a while since he had seen her, although he often thought of her. Woody continued about his day at the races. Lenny, half listening, thought about Dana as he put his papers in the proper order for his lecture tomorrow.

CHAPTER 5

> Accounting is the process by which the profitability and solvency of a company can be measured. Accounting also provides information needed as a basis for making business decisions that will enable management to guide the company on a profitable and solvent course.
>
> — Meigs and Meigs

Frank Harrison was scheduled to testify for Jane Braswell in the Superior Court of Philadelphia. She was the wife of a wealthy heart surgeon in Philadelphia. Frank did a great deal of divorce work for attorneys, but few of them ever reached the courtroom. This messy marital split-up was the exception. Frank felt qualified to testify about the valuation of a service-type business, plus Benjamin Braswell had an extensive collection of jade carvings and rubies.

Nothing today could be as dramatic as yesterday afternoon. Frank had been in the courtroom waiting to be called to testify. A morning newspaper article best described the bitter dispute as follows: "Tales of Money, Sex, Intrigue Spice Up Braswell's Divorce Drama."

Apparently Jane Braswell had signed a prenuptial agreement with Benjamin Braswell, which limited Jane to twenty percent of the money made by the 48-year-old heart surgeon. A major question of this trial concerned the validity of the prenuptial agreement.

Frank watched a Mrs. Daniels testify about her sexual encounters with Ben Braswell. She said that the sexual events took place during lunch hour at her house while her husband was working at the same hospital that employed Ben Braswell.

Frank was watching Jane Braswell toy with a gold bracelet when Mrs. Daniels complained that she was having difficulty breathing because it was so tense in the courtroom.

Suddenly Mrs. Daniels fainted and fell out of the witness chair. The judge cleared the courtroom, and paramedics arrived. As the paramedics were carrying the woman through the crowded Superior Court hallway on a stretcher, she began screaming.

A few minutes later Jane Braswell's attorney approached Frank, who was sitting in the witness chair. The jury was to the left of Frank and the judge to Frank's immediate right. "Mr. Harrison, have you testified in divorce cases in the past?"

"Yes, about eight such cases."

"Would you please state your credentials?"

Frank leaned forward in his seat and began. "I am president of Quaker City Consulting, the largest consulting firm in Philadelphia. We specialize in valuations, pensions, insurance, and employee benefits.

"I am a Certified Financial Planner — CFP for short — and a Chartered Financial Consultant. I am also a member of the International Association for Financial Planning. Several members of my firm are actuaries."

"Mr. Harrison, what is required to become a CFP?"

"A CFP designation is provided to people who successfully complete a two-year study and testing on risk management, investments, taxes, retirement, employee benefits and estate planning."

"Mr. Harrison, what is an actuary?"

Frank smiled broadly and looked at the jury. "Some people maintain that it is a graveyard for dead actors. But — " Several jury members smiled and one older gentleman actually laughed out loud. "But an actuary calculates insurance and annuity premiums, reserves, and dividends."

"Mr. Harrison, do you have any experience with jade and rubies?"

"Yes, I have taken and passed both the diamond and colored stone courses of the GIA — Gemological Institute of America. I am currently a major owner of the Jade and More Shop here in Philly. I purchase rubies frequently in Bangkok, Thailand, and in Burma."

"You have a business degree from Temple University, is that correct?"

"Yes, sir."

"Mr. Harrison, you were engaged to determine the value of Dr. and Mrs. Braswell's assets, were you not?"

"Yes, I was."

"What value did you arrive at?"

"I estimate their total net worth to be approximately $4,666,000. I need, however, to explain how I arrived at this figure."

"Please proceed, Mr. Harrison. I believe you have prepared some charts for the court."

Frank turned to the judge and asked, "May I move the charts in a position so I can show them to the jury?"

"Please do," the judge said, pointing to the stand with the cardboard charts.

Frank moved the stand closer to the witness chair in a position so that the jury members could see his charts. Frank then handed the judge a copy of the charts.

"Objection, your honor. May we see what the witness has given you?" the opposing attorney almost shouted.

Frank handed another copy to the judge and said, "Here is an identical copy for the attorney."

After the theatrical outburst was over, Frank removed the top blank cardboard to reveal the first chart showing the total estimated value of the Braswells' assets:

Cash	$ 12,700
Accounts Receivable	4,200
Marketable Securities	64,500
House	287,000
Autos	48,000

Business	3,800,000
Jade/Ruby Collection	470,800
Miscellaneous	7,800
Liabilities	(29,000)
Net Worth	$4,666,000

Frank allowed the jury members to absorb the total net worth figure in very large blue numbers near the bottom of the slick, professional-looking visual aid.

He then explained, "Dr. Braswell was not co-operative. My firm had extreme difficulty getting reliable information from Dr. Braswell, especially with respect to his medical practice. Let me start with cash first." Frank gestured toward the chart.

"There may be more than $12,700 of cash available, but this is the figure at about the time Dr. Braswell moved many of the records from the Braswell home.

"The current value of the receivables — $4,200 — is the discounted amount of cash we estimate will be collected using appropriate interest rates at the date Dr. Braswell left Jane Braswell.

"The marketable securities were valued at estimated current market price.

"The house is valued at $287,000, which is what the Braswells could realize from its sale — the estimated sales proceeds, net of brokerage and closing costs. We used a certified appraiser.

"The automobiles are based upon their blue book value, taking into consideration their condition and mileage." Frank pointed to the $48,000 figure.

"Dr. Braswell's closely held business is probably worth at least $3.8 million. Mrs. Braswell had first-hand knowledge of the weekly cash flow into his business. Therefore, I used the cash flow method. This method considers cash flow to Dr. Braswell from his business in excess of compensation that has to be paid to his employees. I calculated six years of cash flows and year six is considered the future value of a perpetual annuity for all later years. Since Dr. Braswell is young, I projected cash flow for twenty years, using a discount rate of eleven percent." Frank turned to the second chart, showing the cash flow calculations. The nodding jury members did not seem interested in the numerous calculations.

"Now for the jade and ruby collection. Dr. Braswell removed the jade collection from the home during the night that he moved away from home. He also took all of the rubies from the family safe deposit — "

"Objection, your honor. My client asserts that Mrs. Braswell removed and hid the jade and ruby collection."

"Objection sustained. Please strike the last statements from the record." The judge waved his right arm at the court reporter. "Mr. Harrison, please limit your remarks to the appraisal and avoid any extraneous remarks."

"Yes, sir. I apologize to the court." Frank tried to look humble. "Anyway, Mrs. Braswell does have photos of many of the jade items, and I sold many of the items to Dr. and Mrs. Braswell — usually Mrs. Braswell." Frank paused and looked toward the jury box.

"The same for the rubies — most of them had been valued for insurance purposes. Using the photos, invoices, and my personal knowledge of the jade and ruby markets, I estimate their current value to be $470,800." Frank turned to a summary chart of many of the most valuable pieces.

"There is approximately $7,800 of miscellaneous assets, and I estimated payables and liabilities at the discounted amounts of cash to be paid. After deducting the $29,000 of liabilities, the total current net worth of the Braswell family is at least $4.6 million — quite possibly much more."

Dr. Braswell's attorney then began to question Frank in a thick Irish brogue. "Mr. Harrison, why did you not use the market comparables approach to value Dr. Braswell's medical business?"

"Well, I considered the market comparables approach, but

decided not to use it because a Judge Nims, in a 1987 Tax Court decision, rejected the use of market comparables approach. However, even using this approach, you'll get almost the same value."

"Mr. Harrison, why did you not reduce your value of the company by a lack of marketability discount — say 30 or 40 percent?"

"I don't believe it is appropriate to reduce the cash flow valuation by any type of discount. We are looking at the cash flow to be earned by a service company. The company's cash flow is based upon Dr. Braswell's efforts. I don't expect him to stop working. If he does, the company is worth little. You would use a discount factor more readily in a non-service, closely held business. Keep in mind that under the cash-flow approach, I did not place a value on Dr. Braswell's goodwill — goodwill is an intangible asset. If you feel a discount is necessary, we need to inflate the value by a goodwill factor." Frank smiled in satisfaction at the attorney. Although Frank knew that the rewards were great in business valuation situations, it did expose him to the risk of litigation. Some professional liability coverage explicitly excludes valuation work.

CHAPTER 6

> Most accountants are dull bean counters without many new ideas. Business needs creativity, innovation, and the willingness to be bold.
>
> — Richard Rampell

Lenny stepped off the bus at Seventeenth and Chestnut and took a deep breath as he proceeded down Chestnut Street. It was a beautiful day for early September in Philadelphia. It was 72 degrees with a mild breeze and bright sun. Absent was the oppressive humidity that can make Philadelphia so unbearable in the summer.

Lenny was still uncertain of his plan, so he wanted to walk a few blocks to calm his nerves. He saw the Philadelphia Stock Exchange in the distance and thought about stopping in and talking to Bill Nicholson, a friend of his who was a bond dealer. He decided not to. It was hard for Lenny to believe that Bill was a bond dealer. Lenny had to explain to him that a bond sold at a premium if the market rate of interest was less than the rate of interest paid by the bond, and that if the market rate was greater than the bond rate, the bond sold at a discount. Lenny wondered if he would be able to smile later on in the day if he went through with his plan as his mind shifted away from Bill Nicholson.

So wrapped up in his thoughts was Lenny that he was oblivious to things going on around him. At Twelth and Chestnut, he almost ran into a mounted patrolman's horse. At Thirteenth and Market, he completely ignored the giant clothespin statue.

As Lenny approached Jewelers' Row, he could feel a cold sweat on his hands. He had been thinking about Dana on a more constant level ever since their last encounter. His big fear was being utterly embarrassed and humiliated. He had an alibi for showing up, but he knew that Dana was probably smart enough to see through it.

Calling upon some inner strength, Lenny decided to go through with his plan. He opened the door and walked in.

"Yes, sir. What can I help you with today?"

Lenny turned and was disappointed to see a neatly dressed blond-haired man of about twenty-eight years of age with a pleasant smile greeting him. It never dawned on him that Dana might not be there. "How stupid could I have been?" he thought to himself.

"Uh, I, uh, well, I'm looking for, uh, a locket," struggled Lenny in a low voice.

"Lockets are a very popular item. If you'll walk this way to our display, I'm sure you'll be able to find something that will fit your tastes," beamed the salesman confidently.

Lenny looked around. There was no other person in the store and no sign of Dana.

"Now tell me, sir, who is the locket for?" inquired the salesman. "Is it for your wife, lady friend, mother — "

"It's, uh, for my daughter for her birthday," replied Lenny.

"That's a wonderful gift for a daughter. I know she will treasure it."

"I hope so," uttered an unenthusiastic Lenny.

"How old a young lady is she?" the salesman inquired.

"She'll be fourteen on September 8," came a voice from behind Lenny.

Lenny turned around quickly and saw a smiling Dana. "That is right, isn't it? Rebecca is going to be fourteen, isn't she?" asked Dana in a manner which suggested that she already knew she was right.

"Why, uh, yes. That's right. But — "

"Excuse me a second, Professor Cramer. Phillip, I'll take

care of Professor Cramer. Why don't you help Janet with the aging of our receivables," Dana suggested in a pleasant tone.

"Whatever you say, Dana. Nice meeting you, sir." The salesman walked behind a purple curtain into a back room.

"How did you know Rebecca was going to be fourteen on September 8?" Lenny asked in astonishment.

"She told me in Burma."

"Yes, but how did you remember?"

"I have a good memory. In fact, I have a *good* memory," replied Dana in a stern tone.

"I'm impressed that you know about aging receivables," said Lenny in an upbeat tone as he quickly changed the subject.

"It was Frank's idea. It is really pretty easy to implement. All one has to do is categorize all one's accounts receivable by the number of days they are outstanding. The longer they are outstanding, the less likely they are to be collected. Each category has a percentage associated with it determined by Frank. The percentage represents the percentage of accounts receivable outstanding for that period of time that are generally uncollectible. The total amount estimated as uncollectible is then compared with the amount already in the allowance for bad debts account. The difference represents the bad debt expense for the period."

Lenny smiled. "I wish all my students were as smart as you. Of course, the whole purpose of estimating bad debt expense is to allow the cost of credit sales to be matched in the same reporting period with the revenues they generate. You know, of course, that the allowance method is no longer available for tax purposes — only the specific change-off method."

There was a long pause. Dana was staring at Lenny. Lenny, in the meantime, with his head down, appeared to be studying a glass display case of chains and lockets. Only the hum of the fluorescent lights overhead could be heard. Dana decided to break the silence. "Well?"

Half startled, Lenny replied, "Well, what?"

"Well, have you decided upon a locket yet for Rebecca?"

"Oh, that. Well, uh, what do you suggest?"

"These over here are quite nice for a fourteen-year-old girl," said Dana, pointing to a group of lockets in the glass display case.

"Yes, they are nice," repeated Lenny in a low tone.

Once again there was a long pause, although not quite as long as before. Dana again was the one to take charge and break the silence. "This is rather out of the way for you, isn't it? If you wanted to buy Rebecca a locket, there are shops much closer to you than my shop. Why did you choose my shop?"

Lenny paused and swallowed hard. "I happened to be in the neighborhood, and I knew that you were honest, and that I wouldn't get cheated."

"How do you know if I'm honest?" Dana said. "For all you know I might be a jewel thief. Have you checked with the police? After all, you don't like to take chances."

"You are honest, aren't you? I can't imagine you being a crook," said Lenny innocently.

"Why not?"

"Well, I don't know. I just always thought of you as honest." Lenny's eyes darted away from Dana, back towards the lockets. "This is a nice one here." Lenny pointed to a silver one.

"I think someone Rebecca's age would like that."

"Well, I'm not sure."

"I didn't think you could make a decision," Dana said.

"I'll take it."

"Don't make me force you to buy it. I wouldn't want to rush you again."

Lenny tried to sound assertive. "You're not rushing me. I think Rebecca would like it."

"Fine, I'll wrap it up for you."

There was a long period of silence as Dana placed tissue paper around the locket and placed it in a box. She then wrapped the box in silver foil paper with a red ribbon around it.

"Will there be anything else?" Dana asked in an impersonal tone.

There was no immediate response from Lenny. Finally, he cleared his throat, took a deep breath and said, "Dana, I haven't been able to put you out of my mind the last few weeks."

Dana looked at Lenny, but Lenny had his head down, only looking up at her occasionally, unable to look her in the eye for an extended time. After finally catching his eye, she replied, "I don't have any problem with us being friends. By the way, Rebecca is going to love that locket."

"I hope so," sighed Lenny.

"So, Lenny, what have you been doing? Have teaching and consulting been keeping you busy?"

"For the most part. The semester is just starting and my consulting work has grown. How are things with you?"

"Fine, I guess." Dana paused and glanced outside the window. "Are you in a terrible rush?"

"No."

"Why don't you come back to my office for a second," suggested Dana. "Phillip!"

Dana called Phillip in from the back room to wait on customers. Dana and Lenny went through the back room to Dana's office. On the way, they passed by Janet, the bookkeeper, who remembered Lenny from the trip to Burma.

After exchanging pleasantries with Janet, Dana and Lenny went into Dana's office and Dana closed the door behind them. "This is a nice office," Lenny was trying to make conversation.

The office had two gunmetal-gray desks. The larger of the two was Dana's. A smaller one was at the far back of the room. Lenny noticed a coffee cup on it with the saying "Love an Accountant; It's Less Taxing." There were no windows in the room, which had a distinct aroma of cigarette smoke. The room was illuminated by overhead fluorescent lights. The dark colored wooden floors made the room appear to be more dimly lit than it really was.

"It's all right," Dana replied smugly. "That desk over there is Frank's. We share the office since there is not much room. I apologize for the smell of cigarettes. Frank smokes like a chimney."

Dana motioned for Lenny to sit down and she sat down behind her desk. Leaning forward, Dana said in a low tone, "Lenny, I know you're busy, but do you think you could spare some time and look at our books? I'm concerned. We're not getting the type of profit I anticipated. Janet and Frank handle the books since I don't know too much about accounting. Frank has given me some very good investment advice, but I don't like being at their mercy. I feel like I'm in the dark. I need someone that I can trust to go through the books."

Lenny's face lit up. "I have a lot going on at the moment, but I think I can come in for a day every other week, if that would be agreeable to you." Lenny pulled his datebook from the inside pocket of his sport coat and wrote a note in it.

"I would really appreciate it if you could," replied Dana, with a note of relief in her voice. "I've been checking some things on my own. I know that sales are up, but my cash profits are down from last year."

"Have there been any large increases in expenditures? New equipment, for example?"

"No more than last year, except for inventory, but that should not be unusual if our sales are increasing, should it?"

"Yes, you're right." Lenny looked up towards the white plaster ceiling in thought. "Maybe we ought to make an estimate of your inventories through the gross profit method. I— " Lenny stopped, turned to his right, and saw Frank Harrison entering the small room.

"Well, look who got lost from his precious ivory towers," interrupted Frank as he entered his office. "I thought eggheads like you just sat around in a library thinking great thoughts all day. What brings you here?"

"He was buying a gift for his daughter, and we were just chatting about our visit to Burma," Dana interjected quickly.

Frank was smiling, but the tone of his voice was biting. "I see. You better watch yourself, Professor. You stray too far from your ivory tower, and you're liable to get those fingernails of yours dirty. Then all of your rich, spoiled students will be horrified at the sight of a dirty fingernail and, heaven forbid, maybe even a callus!"

"I'll be careful," Lenny said, jocularity absent from his voice. "I really should be leaving." Lenny stood up and looked at Dana.

"Sure, Lenny, and I'll give Rebecca a call tonight and wish her a happy birthday."

"You don't have to do that."

"Expect my call." Dana looked sternly into Lenny's eyes, hoping that he could catch her message that she wanted to talk more about the books.

"Okay," replied Lenny with a wink, indicating that he caught the message. Lenny turned to Frank and extended his hand. "Nice seeing you again, Frank."

Frank shook Lenny's hand. "Good seeing you again, too. I hope you don't have to take public transportation back to Penn. You may have to mix with us common folk."

Lenny smiled, waved to Dana and departed. Frank shut the door. Dana looked at Frank and spoke in a stern voice, "Was it necessary to be so sarcastic with him? What did he ever do to you?"

"I don't like the guy. He thinks he knows everything, but in reality he's lost once he leaves campus," grumbled Frank.

"Frank, that's not fair!" countered Dana.

"Maybe." Frank changed the tone of his voice. "What was he doing here, anyway?"

"I told you he was buying a gift for his daughter."

"Well, I don't like that guy hanging around here." Frank changed the subject. "By the way, I looked into those two companies you asked me about the other day. You were right about them being very good investment possibilities. That industry is going to grow quickly."

"Which of the two do you like the best?" Dana asked as her concentration shifted to her investment portfolio.

Frank paused for a moment and then said, "I think you would be better off with Metroblow. It has a better cash-flow statement."

"I looked at that statement, Frank, but how do you gain information from it? I know that a balance sheet reports a firm's position at a single point in time by looking at its resources and debts. An income statement reports performance of a company over a period of time by looking at its revenues less expenses. But I have real trouble following the cash-flow statement."

"Even I have trouble understanding the cash-flow statement," Frank replied, pointing to himself. "Metroblow has a positive cash flow from operations. That means that Metroblow currently is taking in more cash than it is paying out from its normal business activity. With the anticipated growth in that industry, Metroblow should be in a stronger financial position than Cosmogo."

"So the key to the cash-flow statement is to look at the cash flows from operations?" asked Dana as she shifted position in her chair.

"Not entirely. The bottom line is rather meaningless. The change in cash from one period to the next is no mystery. All one has to do is compare the totals from the two periods and take the difference. The key is what caused the change. Was it due to operations, financing activities, or investing activities?"

Dana gave an understanding nod. "I see. If a company had a negative cash flow from operations, then the company in all likelihood has to borrow money to continue operating."

"That's right," said Frank. "Likewise, positive cash flows from investing activities can be a bad sign because it could signify that the company is liquidating its assets."

The two continued to discuss Dana's portfolio and their disagreement over Lenny's presence was temporarily forgotten.

* * *

Lenny went back to his accounting office and worked energetically for three hours on a pressing client matter. Next he sorted through his mail, and three items caught his attention. The invoice for his company's malpractice insurance showed that the cost of the insurance had risen dramatically again. Lenny believed that within a short period of time there would be no small practitioners left in the accounting profession. Their malpractice insurance premiums would be too high, and most of the accounting work would be done by the "Big Eight" CPA firms: Arthur Andersen; Arthur Young & Company; Coopers & Lybrand; Deloitte, Haskins & Sells; Ernst & Whinney; Peat Marwick Main & Co.; Price Waterhouse; and Touche Ross & Co.

Premiums were escalating, coverage was shrinking, and many insurance carriers had stopped all coverage for malpractice insurance. Lenny's insurance premiums had increased by a factor of five within the last three years, while the available commercial coverage had been cut in half. Lenny still remembered what former Chief Justice Warren Burger had said in a speech: "We may well be on our way to a society overrun by hordes of lawyers, hungry as locusts, and brigades of judges in numbers never before contemplated." Burger had been right. There was a stampede of malpractice cases going to the courtroom.

There was a plain white envelope with no return address with a clipping from the classified advertisement section of *The Philadelphia Inquirer.* Someone had circled one particular help-wanted ad:

> FORENSIC ACCOUNTANT This position requires 7 to 10 years of experience in internal auditing, preferably in the banking industry, and/or investigative accounting-type background and experience with IRS or FBI. The successful candidate must have a thorough understanding of and experience with operational procedures, particularly in the area of contractor audits and compliance with agreements. The individual must be able to demonstrate and document familiarity with and identification of suspicious situations, with primary emphasis on fraud detection.

Next Lenny filled out his Continuing Professional Education (CPE) questionnaire. A CPA in public practice has to take

120 CPE hours every three years in order to maintain a CPA certificate. Lenny still needed about six more hours this year.

After three more hours of detailed accounting work, Lenny headed home. Later that evening Dana called Rebecca and wished her a happy birthday. No mention was made of the locket Lenny had bought. Lenny and Dana then talked for about 45 minutes on a number of subjects. Lenny set up an appointment to look at her books.

That evening Lenny drafted an engagement letter to be typed and sent to Dana at Jade and More. The letter made reference to their mutual responsibilities, the general nature of his investigative services, his hourly rate, and information regarding payment expectation. Lenny always received a signed engagement letter from a client before beginning any work.

* * *

"Hello. Lenny Cramer here."

"This is Frank Harrison. How are you doing today?"

"Fine. How about yourself?" It was an automatic response. Lenny was surprised to receive this phone call, since it was obvious from meeting Frank in Dana's office that Frank did not like him.

"Pretty good. I called to apologize about my behavior yesterday. You see, I thought that you were trying to move in on Dana and break up our relationship. She assured me that was not the case yesterday when you left and insisted that I call you today and explain my behavior. I hope you don't hold a grudge."

Lenny was stunned. He had no idea that Frank and Dana were seeing one another. When Dana had called him last night and expressed her distrust of Frank she hadn't mentioned that they were going out together. This changed everything between them, Lenny thought to himself. "No problem," replied Lenny, trying to hide the disappointment in his voice.

"Why don't you come out with Dana and myself tonight for dinner? You can bring your daughter along, too. I know Dana would like to see her."

"That's real nice of you, but I am afraid I can't make it tonight. Perhaps another time." Lenny was just trying to be diplomatic. There was no way he would place himself in such an awkward situation as to go out with a couple when he was alone.

"That's too bad. I hope there's no hard feeling," Frank retorted in a friendly tone.

"No hard feelings. So long."

"Good-bye."

Frank put down the phone, leaned back in his chair and took a puff from his cigarette with a look of contentment on his face. There was a knock on his door and his secretary entered.

"Here are those files you wanted, Mr. Harrison."

"Thank you, Wendy."

Wendy stared at him for a second. "You certainly seem pleased with yourself, Mr. Harrison."

"Wendy," Frank said as he put his cigarette down and stood up from his chair, "I am happy. I just put a great snow job on someone and he fell for it hook, line, and sinker." Frank started to chuckle. "I wonder what I would have done if he had accepted my dinner invitation. Boy, it's a good thing I had him figured out right!"

* * *

Lenny arrived at the jade shop on September 23. It was a Tuesday, and it was a gray, dreary fall day in Philadelphia. Lenny closed his red and blue umbrella, which he had purchased at the University of Pennsylvania bookstore, and unbuttoned his gray London Fog raincoat.

Lenny smiled at Phillip, the salesman, and proceeded to the back room. Lenny felt that his entire experience with Dana was becoming more and more uncertain each time he encountered her. Nothing made sense. Lenny knew he liked Dana, and she had asked him to help her gain some insight into what was causing her cash-flow difficulties. She did not trust the explanations Frank gave her, but she was going out with him. "How could she go out with someone she doesn't trust?" he wondered to himself. Maybe he'd made a mistake in judgment. Maybe Dana wasn't the kind of person he thought she was.

"Hello, Professor Cramer."

Lenny turned around and saw Janet sitting behind her desk with a pleasant smile on her face. "Hi. How's life in the world of bookkeeping?"

"Fascinating as always," replied Janet as both she and Lenny began to laugh. The telephone rang at Janet's desk and provided an interruption that allowed Lenny to exit conveniently and go to work in Dana's office.

Assuming there is no dishonesty, in his past experience Lenny had found that cash-flow problems often start with payables and receivables. The payables deal with the purchase of merchandise from suppliers, and receivables are associated with the granting of credit. Both receivables and payables are tied in to inventory. One other possibility would be the acquisition of property, plant and equipment, which also can use up a great deal of cash.

Lenny decided to go through the payables first. Aside from minor payables for utilities, equipment rentals, and storeplace rentals — all of which were rather constant in amount — the payables largely consisted of five major suppliers. Lenny wrote them down.

East Asian Importers, Inc.
Fred Brown Gem Importers, Inc.
International Jewel Importers, Inc.
Nu-Sang-Wan Gems, Ltd.
Southeast Precious Artifacts, Inc.

Of the five, Fred Brown Gem Importers and International Jewel Importers were the two suppliers with whom the jade shop conducted by far the most business. On the surface, Lenny saw nothing unusual with any of the five suppliers, with one exception. All of the suppliers except one granted credit policies of 2/10, n/30. This meant that the account balance was due in

30 days, but payment within 10 days would result in a two percent discount. Good financial planning can often result in significant savings for a company if it makes a practice of always taking discounts. An examination of the cash disbursement journal revealed that with rare exceptions the discounts were always taken.

The one exception was Fred Brown Gem Importers. Unlike the other suppliers, Fred Brown did not grant discounts, and its balance was due in 15 days rather than the 30 days which was the practice of the other suppliers. Lenny made a mental note to check with Dana as to why they would do so much business with a supplier with such restrictive credit terms.

Lenny knew that accountants did much more than simply keep the books. A good accountant or accounting firm will make recommendations to improve a client's system of internal control. The accountant will typically provide information to the client concerning tax advice and financial planning as well. In short, a good accountant or accounting firm typically will advise the client on how the client can improve its future cash flows. In this regard, Lenny noticed the credit terms granted by Fred Brown even though there was no problem with the accounting for these transactions. In each case, when a discount was taken, the Purchases Discounts account was credited for the amount of the discount, the Cash account was credited for the amount paid, and the Accounts Payable account was debited for its full amount.

Lenny glanced at his watch. It was 4:30. Going through the payables had taken up most of the day. He had hoped to see Dana before he left, but she had told him that she had a dental appointment that afternoon and might not be in the shop. As Lenny began to pack his briefcase, Dana walked hurriedly into the room.

"I tried to get here as quickly as I could," an out-of-breath Dana said as she shook the rain from her umbrella. "But the traffic is bad this time of day. Gee, I hate going to the dentist. They love inflicting pain and making you feel grateful for it. I was so relieved to get out of there that I forgot my umbrella and walked half a block in the rain before I realized it. I don't mean to be so wrapped up in myself. How did it go today?"

With a bemused smile, Lenny was amazed at how Dana was able to spew forth so many words in such a short period of time. "Not too bad."

"Good, let's celebrate my getting out of the dentist's office in one piece by going out to dinner, and you can tell me all about it. I'm starved. I skipped lunch because I was so worried about going to the dentist." Dana put her purse on the desk and began going through her mail.

Lenny paused before replying. "Well, I'm not sure."

"Oh, come on. Live a little, Lenny. I won't bite."

"Shouldn't you see if Frank can make it?"

"Frank!" Dana made a face of disdain. "Why would I want him to come along?"

Lenny put his head down and shifted his feet. "I don't know."

"Good, then, it's settled. We're going to dinner. I hope you like French food, Lenny; there's a great place only five minutes from here."

Lenny grabbed his briefcase and raincoat, and along with Dana headed for dinner. The rain had stopped, so Dana and Lenny were able to get to Le Ciel in a short time. After a brief wait, they were seated. Suddenly Lenny exclaimed, "Dana, I've got to go back to the shop."

Dana looked at Lenny with a startled expression. "Why, what's wrong?"

"I left my umbrella at the shop." Lenny looked at his watch. "I better go get it."

Dana sighed and rolled her eyes. "Really, Lenny, I don't know what I'm going to do with you. Your umbrella isn't going to go anywhere."

"I guess not."

After both had ordered cocktails, Dana leaned back in her chair and inquired, "Well, Lenny, did you find anything of importance today?"

Lenny began fiddling with his napkin. "It's going to take a little time, Dana."

"Oh, I know that. I hope I didn't seem impatient."

Lenny saw the worried expression on Dana's face and tried to reassure her. "No, you weren't impatient. I know you're concerned about your business. Tell me, why do you do business with Fred Brown Gem Importers?"

"Fred Brown Gem Importers? Why, what's wrong with them?"

"It's their credit terms." Lenny put down his napkin momentarily and continued. "All of your other suppliers have credit terms such as 2/10, n/30. Fred Brown only gives n/15."

"I don't understand. What does 2/10, n/30 mean?"

Lenny smiled. "I'm sorry. Sometimes I'm so used to being around accounting people that I forget the jargon I often use is unknown to people outside of accounting."

Before Lenny could explain, the waiter brought over their drinks and took their orders for dinner. Lenny explained to Dana what 2/10, n/30 meant.

Dana nodded her head. "I see. The rationale for granting a discount of two percent is that the supplier feels that by getting the money twenty days early, investments can be made which can make up for the two percent discount."

"Exactly." Lenny resumed fiddling with his napkin. "You really are bright. It's amazing how you catch on to things so quickly."

"No, it's not," Dana quickly replied. "I'm just a natural genius." Dana started laughing at herself, unable to maintain a straight face at her sarcastic comment. Lenny joined her in the laughter. Dana returned to being serious. "I see what you mean, though. The n/15 credit terms are lousy. I don't really know why we do business with him. I'm going to have to ask Frank about it."

"You really should, because you do more business with Fred Brown than you do with any other supplier."

Dana looked surprised. "I've seen the name on a few things, but I never realized we did that much business with him. I'm going to have to check with Frank about him."

"Hopefully, I'll be able to come up with some more after a

few more visits." Lenny began to turn the spoon on the table continuously and put his napkin down.

Dana smiled broadly. "Lenny, you're a real dear for doing this for me." Dana leaned over and planted a kiss on Lenny's cheek. Lenny blushed, and there was a period of awkward silence that was interrupted by the waiter.

"Excuse me, these drinks are from the gentleman seated over there."

Dana and Lenny both looked in the direction indicated by the waiter, where they saw a grinning Frank stand up and begin to walk over to their table.

Frank extended his right hand to Lenny and said as they shook hands, "I sure didn't expect to see you two here. I'm real surprised." Frank looked directly into Lenny's eyes. Lenny swallowed hard. It was clear that Lenny was struggling to think of what to say. Dana came to his rescue.

"Just a social gathering for a few drinks and dinner. No big deal, really. Why don't you join us?"

"Yes, Frank," Lenny said as he finally was able to spit out some words. "Please join us."

"No, thanks. I was on my way out when I saw the two of you. I have some work to do." Frank paused and continued. "So you two just decided to get together here, huh?"

Dana quickly responded, "That's right. Lenny called me and said he was going to be downtown, and I suggested we meet here for dinner and drinks. Isn't that right, Lenny?"

Lenny looked at Dana and nodded in agreement.

"What brought you here, Frank?" Dana asked.

"Oh, I had a late business luncheon with a client." Frank stood up and adjusted his tie. "If you'll excuse me; I must be going. Good seeing you again," Frank said, turning to Lenny.

After Frank quickly walked out of the restaurant, Lenny turned to Dana and asked, "Why did you tell him that story about my being downtown and meeting you here?"

"I don't want Frank to know you're looking at our books. Besides, it wasn't a complete fabrication. You were downtown, and it was my idea to come here."

"I would just hate for him to get the wrong idea," sighed Lenny.

"What do you mean by that?" Dana inquired, eyebrows raised.

"Well, I would just not want him to feel that I was trying to ruin things between you and him." Lenny was in the process of tearing his napkin into little pieces as he spoke.

"I agree. That's why I told him that you and I were meeting socially rather than professionally. I don't want him to know that you are looking at the books, Lenny, because you're right. If Frank knew that you were looking at our books without his consent, our partnership would be over."

Lenny was confused. He was not talking about Dana and Frank's partnership in the jade shop when he spoke to Dana about ruining things between her and Frank. "Maybe she feels that her personal life is none of my business," he thought to himself.

The waiter soon brought them their dinner. Their conversation shifted to talking about Rebecca and life at Wharton. After dinner, they went to their own homes, taking separate cabs.

* * *

Frank left Le Ciel and immediately headed for the jade shop. He hadn't thought Lenny would have the guts to go out with Dana after the phone conversation he'd had with him. He was sure that Dana was having Lenny poke around the books. If that was true, then Frank had to make sure some things were in place. He also had to develop a plan to slow Lenny down if he found out too much too soon.

When Frank got to the jade shop, the street was rather quiet. People were still milling about, but nothing like the large number of people that occupied Sansom Street between 9 and 5. The shop was closed. Frank took out his keys, opened the shop and walked in, locking the door behind him.

Frank walked into the office area and looked to see if anything had been examined. It looked like the payables ledger and cash disbursement journal might have been examined, but he couldn't be sure. Everything else seemed to be the way he had left them. He went through a few more files and books, but saw nothing out of place. Frank was beginning to think that he was possibly jumping to conclusions.

To be on the safe side, Frank wrote down the exact order from top to bottom of all the books in the filing cabinet. This would allow him to know in the future if any of the books were examined. Frank was assuming that no one would be careful enough to place the cash receipts journal for last year three from the bottom after examining it if that's where it was initially. Frank then took out a marker and began numbering some files and documents in sequential order. The writing was not visible to the naked eye, however, and required a special light to become visible.

Convinced that he had properly arranged things in a manner that would allow him to know if anyone was looking at the books, Frank closed his briefcase and prepared to leave. He looked at his watch. He was surprised to discover that he had spent an hour and a half arranging things. He was about to turn off the light when he saw something unusual — a red and blue umbrella. Frank walked over to it and picked it up. He looked at a tag on it which had the price along with "University of Pennsylvania Bookstore." "So he was here," he said aloud in the empty office.

Frank decided not to worry about it for now. If Lenny found anything, he was sure he would hear from Dana about it soon. Now that he knew Lenny was looking around, Frank wanted to make sure that he could control what Lenny saw.

Frank locked up the shop and walked out the door. He was going to go to his consulting office to work on some other things as well as plan what to do about Lenny. The streets were virtually deserted around Sansom Street now, so for safety reasons Frank headed for Chestnut Street, which would have more people on it this time of night. Frank was relieved to reach the more populated and brightly lit Chestnut Street.

"A dollar for a cup of coffee, sir?"

Frank turned to his right and saw a panhandler walking

alongside him. The panhandler had a dirty gray beard and hair to match. He was dressed in rags and smelled of urine.

"Get a job, you crumb. It's because of filth like you that interest rates are so high. Why the government supports people like you I'll never know." Frank had little tolerance for street people and other "leeches of society," as he called them. Frank came from a poor background and worked hard to make himself a success. He could not understand why others did not do the same.

"I got nothing to do with interest rates," the panhandler insisted.

"Get away from me, you leech, or I'll call a cop," Frank ordered. "What does that bum know about interest rates," he thought to himself. Earlier in the day, Frank had calculated the amount of a bond discount to amortize for a client by using the effective interest method. It involved multiplying the book value of the bond by the market rate of interest to compute interest expense. The amount of interest paid was equal to the face value of the bond multiplied by the interest rate of the bond, and the amount of the bond discount amortized was equal to the difference between the interest expense and the cash paid. The market rate of interest was much higher than the interest rate on the bond, creating a very large bond discount account.

"I can tell you about takeovers," the panhandler mumbled.

"What can *you* tell me about takeovers?" Frank stated sarcastically.

"I know things," the panhandler insisted.

"I'm calling a cop."

"I know that MFZ Industries is going to take over Marsupial Services."

Frank stopped and stared at the panhandler. "Where did you hear that?"

"I heard it at lunch today — on Rittenhouse Square. I was going through the trash cans there — you get good things to eat there around lunch. Those people throw out good food — "

"Get back to the takeover," an impatient Frank snapped.

"Well, this man said that he was going to announce his plans to take over Marsupial tomorrow afternoon at 5 P.M."

"What was the guy's name?" Frank asked, sarcasm completely gone from his voice.

"I don't know his name, but the other man called him Vince."

"Describe him."

The panhandler stopped for a second and asked, "Are you going to give me a dollar?"

"Don't worry about the dollar," snapped Frank. "Tell me about the guy."

"He was short with a gray Van Dyke beard. He was bald up top with hair on the side, and he smoked a pipe."

"Vincent Mayville!" Frank uttered in disbelief. "Everyone thought his announcement tomorrow was to announce his retirement. There hasn't been an inkling that he was going to try and take over Marsupial." Frank turned to the panhandler. "Have you mentioned this to anyone?"

"No, not a soul."

"You're not making this up, are you?"

"No, I swear."

Frank took out his wallet. "Here's twenty dollars for telling me this, and here's another twenty dollars not to mention it to anyone else."

"Thank you, sir; thank you. I won't mention it to a soul. You have my word," the panhandler said.

"One other thing," Frank said as he pulled out a card and began writing on the back of it. "Here's my card. If you ever hear of anything like this again, you give me a call or come by my office and show my secretary this card."

"I'll keep my ears open, sir, thank you."

"Great," Frank said, walking away at an increased pace. His priorities shifted for the time being as he began planning how best to take advantage of this valuable information that had been made available to him.

CHAPTER 7

> To the contrary, GAAP is not divine in origin; it is, instead, something of a chimera derived from economics, law, mathematics, the behavioral sciences, ethics, and communications. Over the past forty years the accounting profession has endeavored to codify this body of knowledge.
>
> — Abraham J. Briloff

Dana looked up from her desk when she saw Frank walk into the office. "Frank, I haven't seen you for a week since you ran into Lenny and me at Le Ciel."

"I've been busy."

"Yes, I saw the little item about you in *The Philadelphia Inquirer.* It said you did very well with the takeover of Marsupial."

Frank adjusted his tie, then sat down at his desk and began to sift through some mail as he spoke. "I took a bit of a gamble. I would have included you in it, but there was so much uncertainty involved with the deal that I did not want to run the risk of it falling through and friends of mine losing money."

"Oh, I understand," replied Dana.

"Anything unusual going on here with the jade shop?" inquired Frank as he changed the subject.

"Nothing, really, although I did have a question about something I noticed the other day."

"What's that?" Frank asked as he finished separating his mail.

Dana tried to be very casual in her tone as she spoke. "I

was going through some papers and I noticed that we do a great deal of business with Fred Brown Gem Importers. Why do we do so much business with them when they grant such lousy credit terms?"

Frank immediately put his mail down and glared at Dana. "Fred Brown Gem Importers is the foremost importer of Burmese gems in the country. We could direct more business to others and away from Fred Brown, but we would be lowering the quality of much of our jade goods substantially. We also would lose a significant portion of our clientele who come to our shop expecting the highest quality in jade."

"I was just curious." Frank's icy glare made Dana uncomfortable, and she added, "I felt there had to be a logical explanation. Thanks."

Frank soon departed and shortly thereafter Dana called Lenny on the phone and told him about her conversation with Frank. She mentioned to him how uncomfortable Frank appeared to be about Fred Brown. Lenny said that he would be at the jade shop in two days and would examine the receivables and start on the inventory to see if he could find anything else.

After the phone conversation, Dana called another merchant on Jeweler's Row, Irv Moskowitz. Now 64 years of age, Irv Moskowitz was regarded by some as the Dean of Jeweler's Row. He had continued a business started by his father, and the Moskowitz name had been on Jeweler's Row for over 58 years.

"Hello, Mr. Moskowitz, this is Dana Scott."

"Call me Irv. Everyone else does. How are you today, Dana?"

"I'm fine, thanks. How about yourself?"

"Eh, you do not want to know, my dear."

"What's wrong?" Dana asked with alarm.

"Don't get old." Irv paused for a second. "A young girl like you should be married. You should not run a jade shop and become old like me. Get married. Have a family."

"But you're already taken, and all the other men pale in comparison to you," giggled Dana.

"You flirt with an old man like me. You must have something important to ask me. What is it, darling?"

Dana laughed. Whenever she spoke with Irv he always told her to get married, and she would always express her devotion to him. It was a running joke they carried on continuously. "I do have something to ask you. It is about Fred Brown Gem Importers. What do you know about them?"

"They have very good merchandise, if that's what you mean."

"Is it among the best?"

"It is good, but there are some better. I will tell you, my dear, that we do business with them, and have no complaints."

"What type of credit terms do you get from them?"

"One moment, my dear, let me look that up for you." There was a rustling of papers that could be heard over the phone. Then Dana heard Irv yell, "Sylvia, get me our Fred Brown file." After a few more seconds Irv got back on the phone. "Dana, are you there?"

"Yes."

"Our terms with them are the same as most others — 2/10, n/30."

"2/10, n/30?" Dana repeated in surprise.

"Yes. Is there something wrong, my dear?"

"No, I was just curious to know what you knew about them, that's all," Dana said in consternation.

"The only thing I hear about them, and don't repeat this to anyone," Irv said as his voice lowered to a near whisper. "I hear that Fred Brown sometimes deals with stolen jewelry and smuggled gems. But they do this only with private customers and not with people like you and me. I always check for the title of all the items I receive from them to make sure they're legitimate. I have never had a problem with them so far. Like I said, my dear, that is what I hear; it could be gossip."

"Well, I appreciate your giving me this information. Thanks a lot, and take care of yourself, Irv."

"Now you can do something for me."

"What's that?" Dana asked, anxious to return the favor.

"Make an old man happy and get married."

"You won't give up, will you?" said Dana laughingly.

"Take care, my darling. Good-bye."

Dana looked at the clock on her desk. It was 4:45. It was too late for her to call Fred Brown. She decided not to do anything until Lenny came in on Thursday.

* * *

Frank decided not to wait. He was surprised that Dana had asked him about Fred Brown. He had to do something to slow down Lenny.

Late that night, Frank went back to the jade shop. He checked through the books and files, but they remained untouched since he had placed them in order a week ago. Taking care to notice where he placed items, Frank inserted some documents which he hoped would keep him in the clear. The problem was stalling Lenny.

* * *

Dana looked at her watch. It was 10:03, only a minute later than it was the last time she had looked at her watch. "Where could he be?" she said, aloud alone in her office. She was speaking of Lenny, who was supposed to come by the office around 9:30 on this Thursday morning, but he'd not yet arrived.

Dana stood up and started to pace around the office. She wanted to call him to see what was keeping him, but she felt she could not do that since Lenny was helping her in his spare time as a favor to her. She hoped that he did not take the bus, but drove instead. She became convinced that he was too cheap to pay the parking fee in downtown Philadelphia. "Accountants are so cheap," she thought to herself. He could spend 20 to 30 minutes waiting for a bus, and the buses are not expresses. They stop at every corner. Every accountant she had ever met was the same cheap and a lousy dresser. Accountants looked satisfactory as long as they were in a suit, but keep them away from sport coats. They do things with plaids and pastels that should be illegal.

Dana's thought process was interrupted by a knock on the door.

"Come in."

"Hi, Dana," said Lenny breathlessly as he walked into the office. "I'm sorry I'm late, but I just missed the bus at 34th and Chestnut, and I had to wait 20 minutes for the next one to arrive. It was packed with senior citizens since they can ride free at that time. It stopped at every corner to either pick up people or let them off. If that wasn't bad enough, it took even longer since many of the senior citizens took a long time to get on and off the bus."

"That's okay," Dana replied as she tried to contain her smile. Dana then noticed Lenny's attire. He was wearing a rumpled yellow and black plaid sport coat which looked as if it had been packed in a duffel bag for a year. In addition, Lenny was wearing a blue shirt with green stripes along with a solid brown tie. Lime green trousers and white shoes finished off the wardrobe. Unable to control herself, she turned away from Lenny and started to giggle.

"What's so funny?" Lenny inquired innocently.

"Nothing, really. Just something I was thinking of when you came in," replied Dana sweetly.

Dana told Lenny about the conversation she had had with Irv Moskowitz, and how she planned on phoning Fred Brown Gem Importers today concerning their credit policy. She also told Lenny about the different views expressed by Frank and Irv concerning the quality of the goods provided by Fred Brown and about the rumors of his dealing with stolen and smuggled jewelry.

"I think I know someone who might be able to verify the stolen-goods rumors," Lenny stated as he began to smile at the thought of who could help him. "Who do you think is right about the quality of merchandise from Fred Brown, Frank or Irv?"

"Remember, Lenny, Irv said that Fred Brown had very good things, but that it wasn't the best around, as Frank said. I don't think it's a matter of who is right or wrong, but more of a professional difference of opinion."

"That makes sense," Lenny replied. "I think you ought to call Fred Brown, though, about their credit terms."

"I hate doing that behind Frank's back," replied Dana. "It's possible he could find out."

"It's up to you," sighed Lenny.

"Okay, I'll call," Dana said with resignation.

Dana called Janet to look up the phone number for Fred Brown. Dana then called Fred Brown, but got a tape-recorded message asking the caller to leave one's name, phone number, and a brief statement concerning the objective of the phone call. A customer service representative would call back as soon as possible. Dana left a message, and five minutes later the phone rang, with a customer service representative from Fred Brown on the other end.

"You have a question concerning your account with us, Miss Scott?" the female voice on the other end of the line asked.

"Yes. I want to know why my shop has credit terms of n/15 while other shops which do business with you have terms of 2/10, n/30."

"I'm afraid I can't answer that for you," the customer service representative replied. "You are going to have to speak to Mr. Brown about it, but he's not available at the moment. Can I have him call you back when he returns?"

"Yes. Please do."

After Dana hung up and recounted her conversation to Lenny, Lenny decided to start examining the receivables and asked her to keep him informed. Dana went out to the store to help with some customers while Lenny sat down at Frank's desk and began to look through the receivables.

Lenny started with Notes Receivable, thinking that there would not be too many. The only unusual item was a series of notes received from Fred Brown. The notes were for a wide range of amounts extending over a long period of time. Lenny traced the notes to the Sales Journal and General Journal. About seventy percent of the notes were associated with the sale of merchandise to Fred Brown. Lenny had to examine each individual entry in the General Journal related to the notes received from Brown in order to determine the reason for the other 30 percent. It took quite some time, but Lenny was able to find all of the explanations for the remaining notes. They were for services performed by Brown.

Suddenly, Dana ran into the office. "Lenny, you've got to get out of here. Frank's on his way."

"I thought you said he rarely stops by before four o'clock," Lenny said with surprise.

"Have you been daydreaming?" Dana inquired with a smile on her face. "It's 3:55. I just got off the phone with Frank. He said that he would be here within fifteen minutes."

Lenny had totally lost track of the time while searching for the various notes received from Fred Brown. He began to pack up and hurriedly put the books and files away, disappointed that he did not have the opportunity to look in the files for documentation in the form of a receipt indicating what services the jade shop performed and who performed the services.

"Did you find anything?" Dana inquired as she glanced again at her watch.

"Perhaps. Tell me, Dana, did either you or Frank ever do any work or consulting for Fred Brown?"

"I surely didn't," Dana replied with bewilderment. "I've never even met him."

"Why don't you call me tonight at my office," Lenny suggested. "I'll be working there until eight o'clock. We can talk about it more then. In the meantime, I'd better leave. I don't want Frank to see me here."

Lenny said good-bye to Dana and headed onto busy Sansom Street, whose sidewalks were very congested with people.

Unbeknownst to him, Frank was in a corner phone booth from where he had phoned Dana earlier. He had a perfect view of Lenny departing.

* * *

Frank and Dana chatted amicably for the hour or so that they were together in the office that afternoon. Frank never said a word about seeing Lenny, and Dana never brought up Fred Brown's name. When Dana left, Frank immediately checked and saw that someone had been looking at both the books and the files. It was clear to him that it must be Lenny. Frank knew that he had to slow Lenny down, and he hoped that his series of plans would work.

Frank gathered his belongings, left the jade shop and walked to his car. He lit a cigarette, got into his car and drove to Dorney's Tavern. It was only a five-minute drive, and Frank wanted to make sure that he was there by 7:30 P.M. He parked in a public garage, then looked at the ticket that he needed to present upon exiting. 7:19 P.M. was printed on it.

Dorney's was a place that Frank frequented on many occasions. He knew all of the bartenders and most of the barmaids, so it was not at all unusual that he was recognized and greeted when he walked into the tavern.

"Frank, how are you doing?"

Frank looked at the large man behind the bar who greeted him. Al was about six-feet-four-inches tall and weighed about 260 pounds. He had played football at Frankford High School, but a knee injury his senior year effectively ended his football career. Now, at the age of 32, Al was the head bartender at Dorney's.

"I'm doing pretty good, Al; how about yourself?"

"Not bad. You want the usual, Frank?"

"Fine." Frank sat down at the end of the bar. It was an active night, but not especially crowded. Frank looked up at the television. The college football game was just beginning.

"You going to watch the game?" Al inquired, already knowing the answer.

"You know what a fan of Temple I am," Frank responded.

"They may have a tough time knocking off Akron tonight, Frank."

"Al, there won't be any zip left with Akron after Temple is through with them." They both chuckled over Frank's pun on Akron's nickname, the Zips. "Can you imagine having a nickname like the Zips? You know, Al, it's short for the Zippers."

"Get out of here."

"I'm serious. They were originally called the Zippers and their name was shortened to the Zips."

"I wouldn't touch that line with a ten-foot pole," Al replied as both he and Frank bellowed with laughter.

Frank then saw a tall blonde walk in and sit alone at a table. He looked at Al and raised his eyebrows. "Al, I think I just found a good table from which to watch the game."

"Yeah!" replied Al with a wink.

Frank looked at his watch, and then said to Al, "Hey, Al, can you tell me what time it is? My watch must have stopped."

"It's 7:38."

"Thanks. Make sure you send someone over to the table to serve drinks."

"No problem. Happy hunting."

Frank smiled at Al and walked over to the table where the blonde was sitting, struck up a conversation, and watched the game.

* * *

"Hello," Lenny said, picking up the phone on the second ring.

"Hello, Professor Cramer, this is Fred Brown. Dana Scott said I could reach you here. She suggested I speak to you to explain about my consulting work with the jade shop."

"Sure."

"I'm just around the corner from you in the lounge at the Sheraton," Brown said. "Perhaps you could drop by here, and I could show you some of my papers which detail the work I did."

Lenny looked at his watch. It was 7:25. "I can be there in about five minutes, but I can only spend about a half hour with you."

"That'll be fine. I look forward to seeing you. Dana Scott described you to me so I'll find you in the lounge."

"That will be fine, Mr. Brown. I'll be there in five minutes."

Lenny hung up the phone and gathered his work together, deciding what he was going to take home with him and what he was going to leave in the office. He looked outside the window. It was dark out now.

Lenny began to wonder why Dana had not called him prior to Fred Brown's phone call. He also was curious about what Fred Brown was going to show him. Lenny hoped he might learn something from Fred Brown that would help him solve Dana's problem at the jade shop.

Lenny locked his office door, turning the doorknob several times from habit to make sure that the door was locked. He walked down the two flights of stairs and stepped out the door into the chilly fall night. He walked over to his car, but before he could get in, Lenny was struck from behind by a blunt object. He dropped his briefcase and tried to break his fall, but it was too late. The force of the blow, combined with his head hitting the cement, caused him to lapse into unconsciousness.

* * *

"Look! He's starting to move around. Dad, are you okay? Can you hear me, Dad?"

Lenny recognized Rebecca's voice and smiled. His head was throbbing, and he found it difficult to concentrate.

"Mr. Cramer, this is Dr. Milliken. Can you hear me?"

"Yes," Lenny garbled as he tried to sit up.

"Don't move, Mr. Cramer. Just keep still."

"Fine," Lenny replied. "What happened?"

"We were hoping you could tell us that," the doctor replied as he looked into Lenny's eyes with a light.

"I remember going to my car, and then I remember falling."

"Anything else?" inquired the doctor.

"Nothing else until I heard Rebecca's voice," answered Lenny, squeezing Rebecca's hand.

"Well, you took quite a blow to the head by a blunt object, Mr. Cramer. There was a cut on your head that required six stitches," the doctor continued in a calm voice. "It appears to me that you may have suffered a slight concussion. At the moment I don't think it's serious, but I would like to keep you here overnight for observation."

"Fine. By the way, what hospital is this?"

"University Hospital," the doctor replied. "The police brought you here when they found you on the street. They are going to want to question you about this, but I'll have them return tomorrow. Now I want you to rest."

"Fine," replied Lenny weakly. He felt like sleeping to relieve the pounding in his head. "Rebecca, I want you to take a cab — "

"That's not necessary, Dad, Dana can take me."

"Dana?"

"She picked me up and drove me here. She's waiting outside in the waiting room."

"How did she know?" Lenny asked.

"She tried to reach you at your office," replied Rebecca. "Then she called our house to try and reach you. Then she called later when you still were not home. She told me to call her if I heard anything. She drove me here. She said I could stay with her tonight. Is it okay, Dad?"

"Sure," replied Lenny, squeezing Rebecca's hand. "Thank Dana for me, and I'll see you tomorrow, Rebecca."

"Good night, Dad. Get better."

"Now, Mr. Cramer, I want you to take these two pills and get a good night's sleep," the doctor ordered.

Lenny complied with the doctor's orders and spent the night sleeping in the hospital.

* * *

Lenny was feeling much better the next morning when the doctor examined him. The doctor told Lenny that he could leave the hospital and that he should go home and rest for about three days before returning to work. Lenny called his department head at Wharton, and arrangements were made for a graduate student to take Lenny's classes. Prior to his discharge, he was paid a visit by Detective Calhoun of the Philadelphia Police Department. Lenny was so tired and concerned about the throbbing in his head that he had not thought about the mugging until now.

"Did you see the person who attacked you?" Calhoun asked.

"No."

"Do you have any idea who it could have been?"

"No."

"Nothing was stolen, is that correct?"

"To the best of my knowledge, no," replied Lenny.

"Let me make sure I understand the episode," Calhoun said, looking at his notepad. "You left your office around 7:30 and were on your way home when you were hit from behind prior to getting in your car."

Lenny nodded. "That's right, except that I was on my way to meet someone and then I was going home."

"Did you notice anyone around the building at all last night?" Calhoun inquired.

"No, I was all alone."

"I wish I could help you out, Professor Cramer, but to be honest with you, I don't see how we can possibly apprehend the individual since nothing was stolen from you and you never saw the person." Calhoun closed his notepad and placed it in his inside coat pocket. He was a large black man about forty years of age. He looked imposing at about six-foot-two in height and two hundred pounds in weight. "If you think of anything else, give me a call at this number." He handed Lenny a slip of paper with a phone number on it.

"I'm sorry I couldn't be of more help, Detective," sighed Lenny. "It just happened so fast."

"It's just fortunate you're fine. So long."

Lenny was discharged from the hospital late that morning. Dana picked him up outside the hospital and drove him to his car, which was still parked outside his office building.

"You know what's a real shame about the whole thing?" Lenny posed after he and Dana had talked about the mugging.

"No, what?" Dana responded.

"I was all set to meet with Fred Brown concerning the work that was charged to him and the notes that you have. I was going to meet him when I got hit."

"What notes?" Dana inquired.

"I forgot," Lenny said with a smile. "I was going to tell you last night about the large number of note receivables you have with Fred Brown for sales and services rendered. That's why I asked you about it yesterday."

"How did you get in touch with Fred Brown? I called there yesterday, and they never returned my call. I'm going to have to call him again," Dana said as she parked behind Lenny's car.

"Wait a minute!" Lenny exclaimed incredulously. "Fred Brown never called you back?"

"No."

"He told me he spoke to you."

Dana shut off the engine and turned towards Lenny. "He never spoke to me." There was a brief period of silence before Dana continued. "Did he say that when he called you last night?"

"Yes. In fact, he told me that you told him to call me."

Dana paused again in anguish. "Oh, Lenny, are you thinking what I'm thinking?"

"What's that?" asked Lenny.

"That the attack last night was no accident. That Fred Brown was the one who hit you over the head." Dana looked pale and moisture began to form around her eyes. She took a handkerchief and dabbed at her eyes.

"That's entirely possible," Lenny responded with some anger in his voice.

"I'm scared, Lenny," Dana cried. "Who knows what he might do next?"

Lenny tried to console her. "If he wanted to do more harm to me, he could have done it easily. If it's him, I think he only wanted to scare me off, not to harm me seriously."

"I feel so guilty," Dana insisted. "I was the one who got you into this, and now look what's happening!"

"Don't worry, Dana. I'm going to call Detective Calhoun when I get home and tell him about this. I'm sure that he will take care of Fred Brown." Lenny unfastened his seat belt and opened the car door.

"Promise me you'll be careful," Dana implored as she gripped Lenny's hand tightly.

"I promise." Lenny looked into the worried eyes of Dana. "By the way, Dana, I appreciate your looking after Rebecca last night and bringing her to the hospital."

"No problem," Dana whispered.

Lenny leaned over and kissed her on the cheek and quickly got out of the car. He walked over to his car and started it up. Dana rolled down the window of her car and shouted, "Make sure you get plenty of rest." Lenny waved, drove off and headed home.

There was not much traffic at that time of the morning, and Lenny was home within ten minutes. It felt good to get back into his house. He had missed the comforts of home during his brief stay in the hospital. He walked over to his desk and looked at his familiar AICPA desk set. Sitting down at his desk, Lenny picked up his phone to call Detective Calhoun. He was pleased to hear Calhoun's voice on the other end.

"Detective Calhoun, this is Lenny Cramer. I have some information that might be useful."

"What is it?"

Lenny told him about the Fred Brown phone call and the subsequent discrepancy with what Dana had told Lenny. Calhoun thanked Lenny and told him that he would keep Lenny informed. Feeling slightly fatigued, Lenny relaxed in an overstuffed chair and read the latest issue of *The Journal of Accountancy.*

* * *

"Frank, I didn't expect to see you here so early today!" Dana exclaimed upon seeing Frank as she walked into her office.

"I have a business meeting later in the day, and I also wanted to talk to you," Frank said sternly.

"What about?" Dana asked with caution.

Frank took a deep breath and looked at Dana sincerely. "Last evening around 6:15, I received a long-distance phone call from Tucson, Arizona. Fred Brown was returning a phone message that he got from his secretary saying that you had phoned him earlier in the day about the credit terms we are receiving from him."

Dana was stunned. Frank had caught her red-handed checking on Fred Brown. On top of that, he had said that Fred Brown was in Arizona. That would have prevented him from hitting Lenny.

"I told him that you called by mistake," Frank continued. "You see, Dana, I know that he gives better credit terms to others, but he gives us his best merchandise. In exchange for giving us first crack, I agreed to the tougher credit terms. As a partner, I didn't need you to agree to the arrangement because any contract signed by one partner is binding on the entire partnership. But I should have told you about it. At the time I agreed to the arrangement, I intended to tell you, but I forgot about it. I agreed to it without consulting you because I thought you trusted my judgment. I had to agree to it on the spot, Dana; otherwise he might have taken the proposition to someone else."

Dana felt embarrassed. "I'm sorry, Frank. I hope you forgive me. You say that Fred Brown called from Tucson?"

"Yes. He called from the Holiday Inn there. Why?" Frank inquired.

"Nothing, really. I always wanted to travel to Arizona," lied Dana.

"There's one other thing we have to discuss," Frank continued. "If you are not going to trust me, then we should end our partnership. This is a hobby for me, Dana. It's certainly not my meal ticket. I don't want to be included in a partnership where my partner is checking up on me. We can end it right now, disposing of the assets and sharing the gains and losses in the same fashion that we have shared profits in the past. It's up to you."

Dana felt extremely awkward. She did not trust Frank, but she was not in a financial position at the present time to buy him out. Like it or not, she knew that she could not afford to have Frank end the partnership at the present time. "No, Frank, I trust you, and I apologize for questioning your judgment."

"Well, that's what I was hoping you would say," Frank responded.

Frank gathered his work and packed it up in his briefcase as he prepared to leave for his consulting office. As he went from the jade shop onto Sansom Street, Frank smiled broadly and said aloud to himself, "Frank, you're a genius."

* * *

"Hello," Lenny said between yawns as he picked up the ringing phone.

"How are you feeling, Lenny?"

Lenny recognized Dana's voice and smiled. "Pretty good."

"I was just talking to Frank. I'll tell you about the whole conversation later, but the most important thing is that he got a phone call last evening from Fred Brown."

"Did Frank get mugged, too?" mused Lenny.

"No," replied Dana.

"Too bad," retorted Lenny.

"This is serious Lenny," Dana giggled. "Fred Brown called Frank from Tucson, Arizona, from the Holiday Inn there. Fred Brown could not have been the one that attacked you!"

"He could not have attacked me, but he still could have called me and had someone else attack me."

"I didn't think of that," admitted Dana.

Lenny thanked Dana for calling and told her that he would call Detective Calhoun about the latest development. While he was looking for Calhoun's phone number, the telephone rang, with Calhoun on the other end.

"I was just going to call you," Lenny stated. "I found out that Fred Brown was in Tucson, Arizona, last night."

"I know," Calhoun replied. "We've cleared him completely. He did not even call you from there. The only long-distance call he made was to Jade and More."

"That's how I found out he was in Arizona," Lenny interjected.

"I do believe I have a suspect, Mr. Cramer," Calhoun added.

"Fantastic! Who is it?"

"Dana Scott."

CHAPTER 8

> The only act which a CPA can perform, and which is denied to all others, is the rendering of an opinion on the fairness of financial statements. The audit function has, more than any other activity performed by CPAs, bound the profession together during its first century.
>
> — Stephen A. Zeff

"Dana Scott!" Lenny repeated incredulously. "That's ridiculous! She — "

"Before you jump down my throat, hear me out," Calhoun said in a calm voice.

Lenny felt like hanging up on the spot or asking Calhoun where he got his police training. The thought of Dana being the one behind his mugging was totally incomprehensible to him, but he decided he would listen to Calhoun. "I'll hear you out, Detective Calhoun, but I'm telling you right now that the thought of Dana being the prime suspect is ridiculous. There is no way she could possibly be the one."

"I'm not saying she's guilty," cautioned Calhoun. "I'm only saying that she is our prime suspect. There is a whole lot of difference between being a suspect and being guilty. The evidence makes her a strong suspect."

"What evidence?" Lenny asked.

"I grant you, it's circumstantial," Calhoun emphasized, "but hear me out. The only ones to know that you were working in your office were your daughter Rebecca and Dana Scott. Right?"

"Right."

"Fred Brown had no way of knowing who you were and your connection to Jade and More unless Dana Scott told him. Right?"

"Right."

"No one else could have known about your interest in Fred Brown. You and Dana Scott were the only ones who could have known that a phone call from Fred Brown to your office would interest you."

Lenny felt uncomfortable. "Maybe her partner found out."

"You mean Frank Harrison? We're in the process of checking him out. At the moment he appears to be in the clear. We know he was in a bar last night at the time you were mugged," Calhoun said.

"You didn't let him know that I was working for Dana, did you?" a worried Lenny asked.

"No," replied Calhoun. "We can be very discreet when we have to be. But let's say that Frank Harrison did find out about your interest in Fred Brown; how did he know you were in your office last night at that time without Dana Scott telling him? I also don't see how Frank Harrison could know of your interest in Fred Brown without Dana Scott telling him. In short, either Dana Scott is involved, or she is lying to you about whom she has told about your involvement. Of that I feel fairly confident."

Lenny did not know what to say. There was a long pause and all that could be heard on the phone was occasional static. He could not argue with Calhoun that Dana was either lying or involved. Then it came to him. "How about Dana's bookkeeper, Janet? She has seen me go in and out of the jade shop. So has Phillip, the clerk. They could have mentioned it to Frank—"

"But none of those could have tied you to Fred Brown," interrupted Calhoun, "and none of them knew that you were in your office last night. We're still going to check them out. Listen, Mr. Cramer," Calhoun's voice became calmer, "I want to repeat that Dana Scott may not be guilty. She may have mentioned something and was overheard by someone else. But, just looking at what we know at the moment, she appears to be involved. Now normally, it is not departmental practice to provide a victim with information concerning a suspect. But, in this case, since you have frequent contact with the suspect, we would rather be safe than sorry. I would recommend that you be extremely cautious when in Dana Scott's presence. It might be wise to avoid her until this thing gets settled. There is one thing in Dana Scott's favor, though, Mr. Cramer."

"What's that?" asked Lenny anxiously.

"I haven't thought of a possible motive for Dana Scott to do you physical harm," revealed Calhoun. "Of course, that's assuming that she is acting rationally. If she is under some type of emotional stress, then there is no telling what would motivate her to do different things."

"Keep me informed of anything else that arises," sighed Lenny.

"Be careful, Mr. Cramer," warned Calhoun.

Lenny hung up the phone and sat down in his chair. He did not know what to think. Dana was someone he had trusted to take care of his youngest daughter last night. He had strong feelings for Dana and did not want to believe that she could be involved in his mugging. There just was no motive to convince him that she would want to do him harm. He could not argue with Calhoun's logic, though, and his natural accounting instincts suggested to him that he must be on the cautious side.

The combination of his conversation with Calhoun and his slight concussion exhausted Lenny, and soon he was fast asleep in his chair, perplexed as to what to think about Dana.

* * *

Lenny returned to his office on Monday morning. He was feeling better, and believed that the weekend rest had recharged him. Dana had called to check up on him, but he received no further reports from Detective Calhoun. The entire Fred Brown episode had stayed on his mind over the whole weekend, and Lenny was anxious to begin working on the puzzle when he got to his office.

One of the first things he did was to get in touch with Woody. Most anxious to oblige, Woody leaned back in the extra chair in Lenny's office.

"Woody, I want to call upon your vast expertise to assist me on a very important matter," Lenny said, trying to withhold a smile.

"I'm at your service, sir," Woody replied, twirling his ever-present cigar.

"Have you ever heard of Fred Brown or know anybody who might know of him?" Lenny inquired. "I hear that he may deal in stolen jewelry."

"You've come to the right place, Doc," Woody replied, leaning forward to make a point. "He's bad news, Doc. From what I hear about him in the neighborhood, I wouldn't be surprised if he dealt with hot merchandise."

"Do you know how I could get in touch with him?"

"I know where his warehouse is. It is back in the old neighborhood in Southwest Philly, but I have never seen that guy around." Woody paused and looked Lenny in the eye. "You want to stay away from that character and get better from that conk in the head you took."

"You heard about that?"

"Everyone around here has been talking about it," Woody reported. "What happened?"

Lenny recounted to Woody how he was hit coming out of the building after receiving the phone call, and how Calhoun suspected Dana of being behind the attack.

"I think the dame's involved," Woody said.

Lenny refused to accept that Dana had played a role in his mugging. "I don't think so. I think Fred Brown is worried about me finding something in his or Dana's records. I don't know how he found out about my activities or whereabouts, but I don't think Dana's intentionally involved."

Woody turned both ways to make sure no one was within

earshot and said to Lenny in a near whisper, "Doc, I can get us in that warehouse if you want to look around. I know the guard there, and if we agree not to take anything, he'll let us in."

"When do you think we could get in?" Lenny asked anxiously.

"Probably tomorrow night around ten. One thing, though," Woody warned.

"What's that?"

"You can't tell that lady anything about this. If you're wrong and she is involved, I don't want Fred Brown having a reception committee for us," Woody said with caution.

"Fine, Woody, tomorrow night at Fred Brown's warehouse."

* * *

Dana put down a jade dealer's advertisement she had received in the mail and began to pace in her office. Dana felt that things were getting out of control. She liked to be in control of situations, but she believed that the events of the past weeks were speeding recklessly out of control.

She had grown fond of Lenny and had felt true pangs of anxiety when he was mugged outside of his office. She was not sure of her feelings about Lenny, but she noticed that Lenny seemed very distant each time she spoke to him since he was attacked. She also felt responsibile for Lenny's being injured. She had convinced Lenny to look at her books and records with the intention of finding a solution to her cash-flow shortage. She never dreamed that she would be placing Lenny in physical danger.

She glanced over at Frank's desk and shook her head in disdain. She didn't believe a single thing Frank had told her about the arrangement the jade shop had with Fred Brown. She privately believed that Frank was getting some type of kickback from Fred Brown in exchange for Fred Brown being a supplier. She had heard of similar situations in other industries and thought it could be happening to her. She also knew that it would be most difficult to prove. "If only Lenny hadn't been hurt," Dana groaned aloud to herself.

She looked at the large wall calendar, which had a different type of jade carving on it for each month. She knew that it would be some time before Lenny would be able to come by and look through things again. She also knew that it would be far more difficult for Lenny to spend any extensive time here during the day, because Frank's suspicions were aroused. She felt that drastic action would be needed if she were going to gain control of the situation.

She walked over to Frank's desk and began to go through the drawers. She didn't know what she was looking for, but she just felt that she had to do something. All she saw, however, were a great deal of papers that dealt with the business but that did not appear to be of much importance.

Dana decided to start taking inventory. Lenny had asked her to do this when she got a chance. Dana figured that the work would help to ease her restlessness.

Frank had implemented the specific identification method cost flow assumption of inventory. Dana knew that FIFO stood for first-in, first-out. The first items purchased were the first ones sold under the FIFO assumption. It would be appropriate if one were selling fresh produce, in which case the owner would want to sell the older produce before it spoiled. Consequently, the first items in were the first sold and the last items purchased were the ones which remained.

Similarly, LIFO represented last-in, first-out. The last items purchased were assumed to be the first ones sold. LIFO would be appropriate if one were in the business of selling coal. As new coal was acquired it would in all likelihood be placed on top of the old coal pile because there would not be the same concern about spoilage with coal as there would be with produce. The coal that would be sold would come from the top of the pile, meaning that the most recent acquisition of coal would be the first coal sold. The cost flow assumption for LIFO is the exact opposite of that of FIFO.

The weighted average cost flow assumption takes the total cost of goods available for sale (beginning inventory + purchases) and divides that total by the number of units available for sale to arrive at an average cost per unit. This average cost per unit is then multiplied by the number of units in ending inventory in order to calculate the cost of ending inventory.

Lenny had also told her that in a period of rising prices, use of the FIFO method presented the highest reported income of the three methods, and that LIFO presented the lowest total under those circumstances. LIFO would be preferable under rising prices since its use results in the lowest reported income. The lower the reported taxable income, the less one has to pay in taxes to the government.

Dana knew that they had no choice but to use the specific identification method of inventory rather than the more prominent FIFO, LIFO, and weighted average methods. One can use these methods only when dealing with inventories which consist of many of the same goods. Their jade shop did not have many items which were identical. For the most part, each item was unique — meaning that no cost flow assumption was necessary. Instead, the specific identification keeps track of every single item of inventory and how much each one cost.

The use of a computer helped to ease the task of using this method. Rather than having to search through the books for the original cost of each inventory item to find its cost, Dana could instead punch in the computer code of the item in the computer, and within seconds the cost of the item, when it was purchased, from whom it was purchased, and a brief description of the item appeared on the screen.

Dana walked around the store writing down the code number of each item in the shop. For the most part they were on the bottom of the merchandise beside the price. It took a long time, since every single code number had to be written down. She could not simply count all the items as one could under the other three methods.

By five o'clock, Dana had finished two-thirds of the inventory. She hoped that the information would be useful in finding out the cash-flow problems, but she also hoped that she would be able to see Lenny soon.

She picked up the phone and called Lenny's office, but got no answer. She then tried to reach him at home.

"Hello."

Dana recognized Rebecca's voice immediately. "Hello, Rebecca. How are you? This is Dana."

"I'm fine, Dana. I bet you're looking for my father."

Dana could hear the rising tone of affection in Rebecca's voice. She knew that Rebecca liked her, and she had grown fond of Rebecca. "You're right, Rebecca."

"You just missed him. He's going out tonight with someone."

"Oh." Dana was stunned. She had never felt that Lenny's drifting away from her was because of another woman. Dana felt that Lenny might hold her responsible for his mugging. She felt very hurt.

"He said he was going to be late," Rebecca continued. "Do you want me to have him call you back when he gets in?"

"No, that's fine," Dana replied in a dispirited voice. "I'll talk to you later, Rebecca. Bye."

Dana put down the phone and walked over to the coat rack to put on her coat. She grabbed her briefcase and left the shop, feeling depressed and sorry for herself as she went out amidst the crowd of people going home from work.

* * *

Lenny took Woody to dinner at a small diner close to where Woody lived in Southwest Philadelphia. It was not a part of the city with which Lenny was very familiar. Most of the homes were either row homes or twins. The houses for the most part were well kept although there was not much in the way of green, elaborate lawns. Those that did have grass rather than cement in front of their houses did not invest in trees or plants. The area consisted of mostly blue-collar workers, many of whom had jobs at the General Electric plant in the area, the nearby Philadelphia International

Airport, or the many oil refineries across the Schuylkill River in South Philadelphia.

Lenny was particularly surprised about two characteristics of the area. One was the horrible conditions of the streets. Potholes were plentiful — there were at least five in every block, and they weren't small.

The other unusual characteristic was the large number of trolleys in the area. It seemed to Lenny that when he wasn't driving around or over potholes, he was driving on or over trolley tracks. There were trolleys on Woodland Avenue, an old run-down shopping area. The trolleys along this route went underground near the University of Pennsylvania and provided service to Center City and the suburbs. There were similar trolleys on Island Avenue and Elmwood Avenue, which were also in Southwest Philadelphia. All three of these trolley lines were within two blocks of one another. Woody explained to Lenny later that part of the reason for all the trolleys was the large number of plants that used to be in the area many years ago. That coupled with a trolley barn designed to house many of the trolleys of SEPTA — the public transportation authority in Southeastern Pennsylvania.

To kill time after dinner, Lenny and Woody went to a neighborhood bar which was a favorite hangout of Woody's. Lenny did not drink much, but he enjoyed watching Woody in his element with many of his cronies.

"They were bums!" Woody proclaimed about the 1964 Philadelphia Phillies baseball team. "Leading by six games with twelve games left to play and they blew it. They're bums. I've never gone to another game since."

"Me neither," a burly redheaded man in his early fifties added. "And Gene Mauch was the biggest bum of them all!" Woody and others nodded their heads in approval.

"Woody," Lenny said in a low voice. "That was nearly thirty years ago. Why are people still talking about it?"

"Because it still hurts, and I'll never forgive them. Right, guys?"

Sounds of affirmation and nods came from the other patrons. Similar conversations went back and forth for another hour, touching on professional football, college football, professional basketball, college basketball, high school basketball and ice hockey.

When the subject turned to ice hockey Woody motioned to Lenny to leave. Although it was approaching 10 P.M., Lenny got the impression that Woody was motivated more by his lack of interest in ice hockey.

Lenny was glad to leave the smoke-filled tavern. He was starting to get nervous about this entire episode. He had never broken into a place before, although this was not really quite the same thing, inasmuch as the guard was going to let them in as a favor to Woody. Lenny wondered if it were worth it. Maybe Detective Calhoun was right. Maybe Dana was involved. Why should he stick out his neck for her? Lenny could not come up with an answer; besides, it was too late to back out now.

They climbed into Lenny's car and left for the warehouse, with Woody giving directions. It was a short drive. The area was so very dark that one did not realize at first glance that the large brick building was a warehouse. Lenny parked his car a block away, and he and Woody walked from there to the warehouse.

The warehouse looked more like a large garage, rather than a typical warehouse. Woody told Lenny that a small taxicab company used to keep all of its cabs inside. Lenny estimated that it could hold about ten cars.

"Don't move!" a voice warned from the dark.

Woody and Lenny stopped in their steps. A flashlight started to beam on their faces. "Hey, Tommy, is that you?" Woody inquired.

"Woody?" The guard flashed his light on Woody's face. "Hey, I thought you two were a couple of winos."

The guard led them into the warehouse through a side door. The light was better. Lenny was shocked when he caught a glimpse of the guard. He was ancient — maybe in his late seventies. The man could not have been much taller than five-foot-four, nor could he have weighed much more than one hundred pounds. It was not the type of guard Lenny had envisioned. He was expecting more of the football-player type.

"Doc, I want you to meet Tommy McLaughlin. He was one of the top lightweight boxers in his day," Woody boasted.

"How ya' doin'," growled Tommy, extending his right hand.

Lenny tried to withhold his smile at the sound of Tommy's voice, which had a gravel tone to it. "Lenny Cramer, pleased to meet you," Lenny said, reaching out to shake Tommy's right hand.

Rather than shake hands, Tommy pulled back his right hand and brought it back over his right shoulder with his thumb sticking out and said, "Go hang it on a wall." Tommy started to cackle uncontrollably. "I told you I'd get him on it, Woody!"

Lenny stared at the scene, unable to conceal a grin. He had heard the expression "Hang it on a wall" in old movies from the 1930s and 1940s. He had never heard anyone use that expression before in his presence. Tommy was clearly getting a big kick out of it, and Woody was enjoying it, too. Lenny really didn't care as long as he got a chance to look around.

"What's that up there?" Lenny asked, pointing to a glass-enclosed room on the second floor visible from the first floor.

"That's an office. You want to have a look?" Tommy asked.

"Yes, please," replied Lenny.

After reminding them not to take anything and to leave things as they found them, Tommy led Woody and Lenny to the office. Woody decided to keep Tommy company while Lenny looked around on his own.

Lenny went to a filing cabinet which contained files on all of the customers. He looked under the letter "S" to see what was listed under Dana Scott's name. It was one of the larger files in that drawer. Lenny opened up the file on the desk and found several invoices for shipments of jade to Jade and More.

Aside from invoices, the only other document in the file was a letter signed by Dana, which indicated her agreement to do business with Fred Brown with the credit terms of n/15 specifically mentioned in the document.

Not seeing anything unusual in Dana's file, Lenny decided to look to see if Frank had a file. There was a large file for Frank Harrison, but nothing dealt with jade. Instead there was a good deal of correspondence concerning a corporation called Browright of which Fred Brown, Frank Harrison, and Speaker of the House Jim Bright were the owners. All of the stock was owned by those three individuals, but Lenny could not find anything which indicated the nature of business in which Browright was involved. Lenny wondered if Dana was aware of the business relationship Fred Brown and Frank Harrison shared through Browright.

Lenny next looked at the payables files to see who Fred Brown did business with. There were not a great many files besides those that dealt with office supplies. Lenny was quick to spot that there was one for Jade and More. In it were copies of the notes that Fred Brown had outstanding with Jade and More. Lenny was about to put them back when he spotted Dana's signature at the bottom of the note. He looked at the other notes. On each of the notes the only signatures were those of Fred Brown and Dana Scott. Lenny was perplexed. Dana had previously told him that she did not know of any services performed by Jade and More for Fred Brown, and that she had never met him. Yet here was her signature on the note. Maybe Dana was not being truthful with him, and maybe Detective Calhoun's contention that Dana Scott was a prime suspect had some merit.

There was another large file for Tijuana Imitation Gem Importers. The file revealed that Fred Brown did a great deal of business with the Tijuana firm, but there was little detail on the invoices aside from the number of items sold to Fred Brown and their cost. Lenny could not find the books of Fred Brown, and was unable to determine for what this merchandise was used.

Lenny could not find anything else in the office that appeared to be important. He looked at his watch. It was after midnight. Where had the time gone? He walked out of the office and saw Woody and Tommy sitting on some crates, talking about the 1964 Philadelphia Phillies.

"Ya find what ya was looking fer?" growled Tommy.

"I don't know," sighed Lenny, walking down the steps. "Would it be a problem if I look in some of these crates?"

"No, as long as you pack everything back up," shouted Tommy.

Lenny started to walk around the warehouse, looking at the address of origin on many of the crates, as Woody and Tommy watched him.

"You need a hand, Doc?" Woody asked. "What address are you looking for in particular?"

"Tijuana Imitation Gem Importers."

"That begin with a T?" Tommy inquired.

Lenny turned around quickly and was stunned to see that Tommy was not joking.

"Here's a couple over here," Woody called, saving Lenny from having to answer Tommy's question.

Woody found a crowbar nearby and carefully opened the crate. It contained various items which looked very much like jade. "Look at this thing!" Woody said, holding up a greenish figure of a squirrel eating a nut.

The other cartons contained similar items. There was nothing in any of them that helped Lenny make any decisions. He kept seeing Dana's signatures on all of those notes.

Woody carefully nailed back the tops of the crates so no one could tell that they had been opened. Once that was done, Lenny thanked Tommy and slipped him twenty dollars for his help. Woody and Lenny then walked outside into the late night. One intruder was tired and the other was frustrated.

* * *

Frank looked outside the window of his office, trying to determine his next course of action. It was a beautiful October day in Philadelphia. There was not a cloud in the sky. The statue of William Penn above City Hall was clearly visible to him. Until the recent construction of some office towers, the statue could be seen from almost any part of Broad Street on a clear day.

The thoroughfare is called Broad Street with good reason. It is an incredibly wide street with many parts having four lanes running in both directions. Most major parades in Philadelphia are held on Broad Street. Frank would often take friends up to his office on New Year's Day to take advantage of its great view of both City Hall and the Mummers Parade, which marched up Broad Street each New Year's Day.

But the Mummers Parade and New Year's Day were far from Frank's mind at the moment. He had discovered last evening at the jade shop that once again someone had been going through things both in his desk and in the books. Frank was convinced that Lenny was the one responsible. Frank was disappointed that the slight concussion suffered by Lenny did not slow down his zeal for examining his books at the jade shop. Frank felt that the time had come for him to play his next card.

"Betty," Frank said over the intercom to his secretary. "Get Bob Hawkins for me on the phone. I believe we have his number on file."

* * *

Dana looked at her watch. It was two in the afternoon, and she finally had taken down all the numbers of the items of inventory in the jade shop, which she had started yesterday morning. She picked up the phone to call Lenny. She had made up her mind that she would not let Lenny's womanizing ways interfere with their business relationship.

"Hello, Lenny, this is Dana. I just finished taking the inventory as you asked. I still have to get a computer output and compare it to the items to make sure that the descriptions match the merchandise."

Lenny was a bit surprised. Dana rarely started a conversation in this manner. She normally engaged in some small talk before getting to the point. He also detected an impersonal tone to her voice. "That sounds good, Dana," Lenny said through a yawn. "Excuse me, I had a late evening last night."

"Yes, I heard. I tried to reach you last night and Rebecca told me."

"You'll be pleased to know that I was working on your problem last night, but I didn't find any answers."

"Don't patronize me, Lenny," Dana said coldly. "You know very well you weren't doing anything last night that had anything to do with the jade shop. There's no reason to lie about it, though. I know you're doing this as a favor in your spare time. I don't expect you to be putting in all types of hours for me."

Lenny thought about what Detective Calhoun had said to him. Calhoun suspected Dana as being his assailant, but could not come up with a motive unless Dana was irrational. She sounded irrational to Lenny now, and he was cautious. "What are you talking about, Dana?"

"Lenny, if you want to go out with a lady friend, you'll get no complaints from me," Dana replied.

"Lady friend? What lady friend? What are you talking about, Dana?" asked Lenny quizzically.

"There's no reason to be secretive about it," replied Dana with decreasing patience. "Rebecca told me that you went out last night and were going to be late."

"I didn't go out with any lady friend," Lenny responded laughingly. "I went out with — " Lenny suddenly remembered his promise to Woody not to tell Dana anything about going to Fred Brown's warehouse. "I went through some old auditing cases to see if there were some approaches to your cash-flow problem that I might be overlooking. They are deep in the bowels of the Law Library and the best time to get to that stuff is late at night," lied Lenny.

"You don't have to be accountable to me," Dana said in a softened tone, feeling embarrassed about her accusation. "I'm sorry if I invaded your privacy. I really did not have any right to do that."

"There certainly is no need for an apology, Dana." Lenny paused for a moment and changed the subject. "So you've got the inventory done. I bet that took a little while."

"It wasn't that bad. When do you think you'll be able to stop by?" Dana inquired, relieved that Lenny had changed the subject.

"I've got a free day on Thursday of next week. In the meantime, compare the computer printout with the merchandise just to make sure that there are no discrepancies." Lenny paused for a moment and then repeated a question he had asked Dana previously. "I think I asked you this before, but just to be certain, did you ever meet Fred Brown or sign any agreement with him for services that either you or Frank performed?"

"I may have signed a contract that Frank gave me for the shop to do business with him, but I've never met the man or done any work for him. Why?"

"And you never signed any notes either?" Lenny continued.

"No." Dana was getting impatient. "Are you going to tell me what's going on?"

"I wish I knew, Dana." Lenny was still cautious about what he said in front of Dana after Detective Calhoun's warning. "I'll see you next Thursday, and hopefully we'll be able to get some things straightened out."

Lenny did not know what to believe. In his heart he wanted to believe Dana. To him, it really didn't matter at this point. His curiosity was getting the better of him, and what he was most concerned about was who was the guilty party. Lenny no longer looked upon himself as working in Dana's best interests, but viewed himself instead as an independent investigator trying to unravel a cover-up of some sort.

CHAPTER 9

> There is a growing evidence in the marketplace that historical cost-basis information is of ever-declining usefulness to the modern business world. The issue for the financial accounting profession is to move the accounting model toward greater relevance or face the fate of the dinosaur and the passenger pigeon.
>
> — Robert K. Elliott

"Hello."

"Hi, Bob. How are you today?"

"Oh, pretty good. How about you?"

"Got a slight problem. Didn't you attend some of Professor Lenny Cramer's classes at Penn several years ago?"

"Sure. Two accounting courses. He was tough. Why?"

"Did you have to write any accounting cases for him?"

"At least three," Bob Hawkins replied over the phone. "Everyone had to prepare three cases for his MBA accounting course."

"Do you still have copies of them?"

"Probably. He always gave them back. Why?"

"Bob, please find them for me. You can help me and make a great deal of money. Do you still have the typewriter that you used at college?"

"Yes, but that's a strange question. What are you up to now? I can always use money."

"I'll tell you tonight at your apartment. Say 7:30. Find the three cases and get your typewriter ready. Go by the campus book store and purchase a copy of Lenny Cramer's new accounting case book — the one used in the MBA course. Can you do that?"

"Sure, why not? Anything else?"

"No, that's enough for now."

"Good-bye," Bob replied as he heard a click on the other end of the line.

* * *

Lenny had set up a meeting with Dean Davidson at 10:00 on Tuesday morning. The dean's secretary had called late Monday afternoon and said that it was important that Lenny talk to the dean. Lenny had a theory that administrators only wanted to see faculty members when there was some kind of trouble. They hardly ever brought good news.

Lenny walked into Dean Donald Davidson's office at 10:03. Don looked up from the letter on his desk, but he did not smile when Lenny said hello.

"Lenny, *you* have a problem. Did you ever have a Robert S. Hawkins in your classes?"

"Oh, I don't know. I've had a large number of students in my classes over the years. I can look it up. I've kept all of my roll sheets since I've been here. Why?"

"This Robert Hawkins came in yesterday and indicated that you copied three accounting cases which he turned in to you three years ago." The dean opened up a manila folder and shoved its contents toward Lenny.

The dean continued, "He left copies of three cases from your new accounting case book. These cases are almost identical to the work which Hawkins turned in to you three years ago. You only changed the names of the companies. How could you be so dumb? You did not even change the names of the people in his submitted work."

Lenny almost shouted, "Wait a minute. I have never copied a case submitted by a student. I always gave them back after I had graded them."

"That was not smart! The student has the original submitted

paper with your grade and corrections on it — in your handwriting." The dean pulled back the photocopied material.

"Look here. The first case involves a company which records the collection of accrued interest separately from the bond proceeds. Don't expect me to understand the way to compute the discount or premiums between interest payment dates, but you copied this student's work word-for-word. Look," he pointed to the first page, "there's your grade. Here you made suggested changes in his wording." Don then reached in his bottom drawer and pulled out Lenny's new book.

Don turned to the first paper clip in the book. "On page 102 you have this same case. You have even made these changes that you had written on his paper. How could you do this?"

Lenny was shocked. He remembered writing the "Deficiency in Accounting for Bond" case. But the handwriting on the student's paper surely looked like his own. There was his distinctive slanted *l*'s.

Lenny looked back at the dean and said softly, "There has to be some simple explanation. I can assure you that I have never copied a student's paper."

"I certainly hope you are right. The student started talking about a lawsuit if you don't give him a cash settlement. I've marked his telephone number on the front of this manila folder. Call him and clear this matter up immediately. We cannot afford this type of publicity. I am suspending you indefinitely until you can settle this matter. I'll get some people to cover your classes."

"But Don," Lenny protested. "You can't . . . "

The dean held up both hands and interrupted, "I have no choice. Settle out of court — and fast. I read every word in your three cases and the student's three graded cases. They are word-for-word. The only conclusion I can draw is that you somehow plagiarized his work. I have to go to a meeting. Please keep me informed as to the status of this *messy* problem."

Lenny knew he was dismissed. He took the folder back to

his office and began comparing the student's papers with the cases in his recently published book. They were identical. The second disputed case involved a medium-sized company that was the victim of a classic liquidity squeeze. The company's sales were increasing rapidly, but so were interest rates.

The third case involved the embezzlement of money from a bank by the chief financial officer. He had simply made monthly journal entries to cover personal expenses paid by the bank. No one had reviewed the entries because the internal audit staff had reported directly to the officer. The internal controls were weak.

Lenny remembered writing all three cases, but he had not retained his pencil drafts. He had long since discarded them. The grades on the three copies of Mr. Hawkins' cases were B+, A−, and B. The markings on the cases appeared to be in his handwriting. Lenny pulled out his roll book, and sure enough, he had given Hawkins these grades on the cases. He had made a B for his final grade. Lenny could not remember the student or the cases. Why had he not kept the submitted cases?

Lenny dialed Hawkins' phone number. He heard a recording, but he did not leave a message. He found Hawkins' phone number in the phone book and jotted down his address on the manila folder.

Lenny compared the student's paper with his published cases. Hawkins' three papers were written too well. But Lenny's handwritten remarks kept jumping out at him.

Lenny had a dreadful thought. Could he lose his CPA certificate? He went over to his bookcase and found the AICPA Code of Professional Ethics. This Code consists of four parts — concepts, rules of conduct, interpretations, and ethical rules.

Turning to the Rules of Conduct, Lenny quickly read through the five enforceable ethical standards:

1. Independence, Integrity, and Objectivity
2. General and Technical Standards
3. Responsibilities to Clients

4. Responsibilities to Colleagues
5. Other Responsibilities and Practices

Failure to follow these ethical rules could result in admonishment, suspension, or expulsion from the AICPA.

Ethical rulings are issued by the Professional Ethics Division Executive Committee. Rule 501 caught Lenny's eye. "A member shall not commit an act discreditable to the profession." A felony, signing a false tax return, issuing a misleading audit opinion, and failure to return client records are discreditable acts.

He had a headache. "I'd better go home," Lenny said to himself. "I have to testify tomorrow."

* * *

"Thank you, Congressman Dangall, for allowing me to testify today concerning your proposal to expand the Securities and Exchange Commission's disclosure regulations. I do not believe there is a need for such an expansion of the SEC's disclosure program."

Lenny was testifying before the Subcommittee on Oversight of Investigations of the House Energy and Commerce Committee, chaired by Congressman John D. Dangall (D-Michigan). These hearings were to review the SEC's role in the supervision and promulgation of accounting standards and to examine the existing structure for establishing disclosure requirements for publicly held companies.

"Professor Cramer," Representative Dangall interjected, "you are aware that Professor Abraham Briloff has indicated before this committee that there is a crisis of confidence in the accounting profession?"

"Yes, sir," Lenny replied, "I am aware that certain people make shrill statements about the accounting profession, but I believe that further disclosure regulations are unnecessary. In fact, I believe that the current large regulatory apparatus is both cumbersome and costly. The establishment of FASB in 1973 was designed to establish standards of financial accounting and reporting. This tripartite structure has lessened the need for governmental regulations. In fact, I believe that the SEC's budget is determined by politicians who are primarily concerned with appearance. This was the position of Professor Watts in 1980 when he stated that the SEC spends a small fraction of its budget on estimating costs and benefits, but that a much larger fraction is spent on lawyers who produce and enforce regulations."

Lenny paused for a moment, then looked at Congressman Dangall and proceeded. "Two major reasons are often given for the need for the regulation of corporate financial disclosures. Both of these arguments are based upon a so-called market failure notion.

"The first argument involves the public-good nature of information. As this argument goes, information for users is underproduced because insufficient disclosure leads to suboptimal resource allocation. Since financial information is considered to be a public good, one may argue that without regulation, an insufficient amount of financial information will be produced."

Lenny raised his voice. "I believe this argument is unfounded. You underestimate both the corporate incentives to provide and the power of market forces to *demand* financial information. There is ample empirical evidence that companies publish financial statements long before they are required to do it. A corporation benefits from disclosure because it is more efficient for the corporation to provide disclosure information about the stock — that is, the product — rather than for the consumer to obtain the information himself. In fact, there is much more likelihood of too much information being prepared — not too little.

"Congressman Dangall, I encourage Professor Briloff and his clones to present empirical evidence that too little information is currently being produced."

"Just a moment, Dr. Cramer. We had a witness yesterday, Frank Harrison, who testified that corporate insiders know much more about their companies than do outsiders. Thus, these unscrupulous insiders may manipulate the stock prices.

Have you forgotten about the many cases in the late eighties when we put so many insiders in jail? Remember Ivan Boesky?"

"Yes, yes, this is the second argument. A manager has an incentive to waste, misuse, or divert corporate assets. Most investors are aware of the incentives for management to act in ways that are harmful to investors. The shareholders must be convinced that the current financial disclosures are accurate and complete. This signaling to shareholders may be done by installing a system of accounting controls and hiring certified public accountants to ascertain that this system is working. The CPA can state whether the financial information generated from the internal control system is reliable. The use of stock underwriters and the adoption of high-dividend-payout policies are two other signaling mechanisms.

"In conclusion, Congressman Dangall, there is no need for additional disclosure requirements. The bottom line is that free market forces induce adequate levels of disclosure and provide sufficient protection for investors. Thank you."

"Professor Cramer, Frank Harrison reported yesterday that the traditional historical cost concept of financial accountants usually causes an overstatement of real income and an understatement of asset values during a period of rising prices. He argued that the current accounting model is deficient when dealing with uncertainty. Can you comment on this gap between historical costs and current values?" Congressman Dangall then smiled as he looked at Lenny.

"Sir, financial accountants have chosen to ignore the problem of changes in value, and they use cost as the predominant measure of value. But historical cost data is relatively objective and can be verified easily. Our built-in conservative bias can be seen in the adherence to the lower of cost or market rule and the postponement of unrealized gains until a realization event — such as a sale or exchange.

"Let me hasten to mention that FASB Statement No. 33 requires the disclosure of current value information on either of two bases — price-level adjusted or current cost. But, surprisingly, surveys of the business and investment communities suggest that users do not find the information helpful. Of course, preparers of such current value information complain that it is a nuisance to assemble.

"Also, Statement of Position (SOP) Number 82-1, issued in 1982, deals with personal financial statements. Now a CPA is required to use the current values of assets and liabilities, with a recognition of applicable taxes, when he prepares personal financial statements. This SOP allows the CPA to use historical cost as supplemental information for personal statements. A client may wish personal financial statements for income tax purposes, to obtain credit, for public disclosure by a politician, for estate planning, and for other reasons."

"Thank you, Dr. Cramer, for your opinion about the deficiencies of the historical cost-basis accounting model." Congressman Dangall stated further, "I believe that companies and investors regard conservative accountants like Dr. Cramer and the type of historical cost information he deals with as of declining utility. May we have the next witness, Sandy Burton, former chief accountant of the SEC and dean of the Columbia Business School."

* * *

Lenny came into his university office, put down his briefcase, turned around and rushed to the Accounting office. He walked into the mail room.

"Hey, Lenny. Have you finished the draft of our stock options paper yet?"

Lenny turned toward Professor Ross and said, "I finished it on Friday. It's in my middle desk drawer. Go on into my office and get it. I need to get my mail, pick up some supplies, and talk to Jim. I'll come to your office in a few minutes. Go ahead and start reading it."

"Good. I have some free time this morning. Did you call Bill Kinney?"

"No. I never caught him in." Bill Kinney was editor of *The Accounting Review,* the top accounting academic journal.

Charles Ross turned and left as Lenny went over to the coffee pot to get a cup of coffee.

Lenny got his university mail and waited outside his department head's office for about three minutes, but Jim continued talking on the phone. Lenny gave up, picked up some letterhead, and decided to go back to his office. "I'll call him instead," Lenny decided.

Lenny's office door was still open when he entered his office. Charles Ross was lying on the floor behind Lenny's desk. Without thinking, Lenny rushed over to Charles, picked up his right arm, and tried to feel Charles' pulse. Before he could feel anything, he heard a loud hissing sound coming from under his desk.

A frightened Lenny saw a pale brown snake lying under his desk. The hissing was rapidly intermittent as the reptile made as much noise as possible with the intake and expulsion of its breath. Three rows of large black rings, bordered with yellow, united to form a chain on the body of the snake.

Lenny jumped backward, ran to his office door, and slammed it shut. He was shaking all over.

For the next hour Lenny was in a daze. The paramedics had been able to remove Charles Ross' body from Lenny's office by using open umbrellas to keep the snake away while they snatched the body from behind the desk. Several times the snake slid more than a foot, jumped and struck an umbrella with its large fangs.

Charles was dead. The paramedics said he might have died of fright after being bitten by the snake. There were two small puncture wounds about three-quarters of an inch apart on his right arm.

A herpetologist from the Philadelphia Zoo arrived and captured the three-and-one-half-foot snake. She told Lenny, "The snake is a Russell's Viper. They come from the Orient."

Lenny called Detective Calhoun, who arrived in about thirty minutes. Detective Calhoun reasoned, "Someone placed the snake in your middle desk drawer during the weekend. Fortunately for you, Professor Ross opened the drawer to get your research paper and was bitten. Someone is trying to kill you." The detective hesitated in order to allow this dramatic disclosure to have its full impact on Lenny. "You must be careful."

"Careful!" Lenny exclaimed. "Can't I open any more drawers until we catch this maniac? What can I do?"

"Well, for one thing, you must sit down and list everyone who might wish to kill you. Have you flunked any Ph.D. students? Are you involved in any fraud cases, with criminals — anything? Think!"

"I believe it could be Fred Brown," answered Lenny.

"How about Dana Scott?" asked Detective Calhoun. "Didn't she go to Burma with you?"

"She was there with the tour, but she's not involved. I can assure you."

"I know, that's what you told me before," Calhoun replied in a disbelieving tone. "But you could be wrong. It's your life. Be careful. I'll let you know as soon as I find out anything."

Later that evening, Lenny told Rebecca about the incident at the university. She went to the bookcase and found a description of a Russell's Viper in the *Encyclopedia Britannica*. She read it to Lenny:

> An abundant, highly venomous, terrestrial snake of family Viperidae. It is found from India to Taiwan and Java, most often in open country. It is a major cause of snakebite deaths within its range. The dreaded viper grows to a maximum of about five feet and is marked with three rows of handsome reddish-brown spots outlined in black and again in white or yellow. Due to its large fangs and the amount of venom expended at a bite, this savage creature is regarded by many toxicologists as more dangerous than the common cobra.

"Gross. Poor Dr. Ross." Rebecca closed the volume and rushed over and hugged her father. Lenny could feel tears on her face.

CHAPTER 10

> Jerusalem, Rome, Benares, none of them can boast the multitude of temples, and the lavishness of design and ornament that make marvelous this deserted capital on the Irrawaddy . . . for eight miles along the river bank and extending to a depth of two miles inland, the whole space is thickly studded with pagodas of all sizes and shapes, the ground is so thickly covered with crumbling remnants of vanished shrines that according to the popular saying, you cannot move foot or hand without touching a sacred thing.
>
> — Shway Yoe

Dana was proofing the letter which she had personally typed to Lenny Cramer:

> Dear Lenny:
>
> This is to formally confirm that you shall act as an accounting consultant for "Jade and More" during the first week in February. I am enclosing a signed copy of your engagement letter. As I have mentioned before, there is a severe cash shortage and/or money is disappearing.
>
> I have told Janet that you will be working on a new inventory system. She is supposed to do whatever you wish.
>
> Frank Harrison left two days ago, and he will be in Tucson during the remainder of this week at the Tucson Gem Show. I shall be in Thailand (Bangkok International Colored Gemstone Association Congress) and

later in the week in Rangoon (Inya Lake Hotel) at the Burmese Jade Emporium. I will fly back to Hong Kong for one day.

Please help me.

Sincerely yours,

Dana Scott
Jade and More

Dana signed the letter, put it in a white envelope marked personal, sealed it, and dropped it into her Gucci purse. On the way to the airport she dropped it off at Lenny's office. He was not there. She attached a note to the envelope: "To my favorite gumshoe accountant." She was worried. Where was the cash going?

On her flight from Philadelphia to Los Angeles, she read several back issues of *National Jeweler,* the newspaper for the jewelry industry. The headline of the latest issue proclaimed "Gemstone Prices Skyrocket As Asians Scoop Up Supply." The gist of the article was that "the supply of gems is diminishing, mainly because Asian buyers are flush with yen and capitalizing on the falling dollar, and are buying up everything in sight."

"Not good," thought Dana. "There'll be a significant increase in my operating expense. The cost of my purchases will increase."

She then skimmed an article about the determination of a jeweler's cash-flow needs. According to the author, her primary business goal centered on the proper cash balance needed for business operations. This figure is the balance necessary to meet the normal, anticipated expenditure requirements plus a reasonable cash safety stock. She computed the formula for the average daily cash flow:

$$\text{Average daily cash flow} = \frac{\text{Monthly cash expenditures}}{\text{30 days}} = \frac{\$30{,}000}{30} = \$1{,}000$$

Assuming a safety stock of six days, her total cash safety stock needs were $6,000. So she needed $7,000 cash on hand each day. She didn't have it.

Dana gazed out the plane's window at the soft, white clouds. "Maybe I should go bankrupt," Dana thought. "Even Texan John Connally, a former Treasury secretary and three-term governor, had gone bankrupt in the late eighties." Dana knew that personal bankruptcy would be declared under Chapter 11, and Chapter 7 could be used for her jade business.

During the morning on her first full day in Bangkok, Dana went to the Grand Palace Complex. Dana especially liked the temples or "wats" in Bangkok because of their colorful, multi-tiered roofs and carved gables.

The Temple of the Emerald Buddha inside the complex was breathtaking. Dana walked inside the main chapel, or "bot," and saw the Emerald Buddha. It was cut from a single piece of monolithic emerald and was 19 inches wide and 26 inches in height (according to the official guidebook). It was sitting high upon a golden throne flanked by other decorated Buddha images. Surrounding this were many offerings from kings, royal princes, and commoners.

The Emerald Buddha was dressed in winter clothes. Dana read in the booklet she had purchased that the king dressed the Emerald Buddha three times a year in the appropriate clothes for summer, rainy, or winter season. According to legend, the Emerald Buddha was given to Nagasena of Patali Putara by God in 43 B.C., and Nagasena then magically placed seven relics of the Buddha into the statue.

Dana was impressed. "More than 2,000 years old," she thought. She knew that emeralds had been selling better in the last seven to eight months than in the past six years. Yet there was a severe shortage of emeralds.

Dana could only get within 30 feet of the statue. Its color was dull grayish-green, and she was reminded of celadon ceramic glazes. The surface glistened with polish which gave it a glassy appearance. She began to mentally calculate how many one-carat emerald rings could be made from the stone.

She stopped calculating. "It's sacrilegious and, besides, it's probably only jade."

On the way back around the Grand Palace Complex Dana went into the Dusit Hall. Here was an audience hall with a throne of mother-of-pearl surmounted by the usual nine-tiered white canopy — the mark of a duly crowned king.

After lunch Dana went to the Dusit Thani Hotel for the Gemstone Congress. It was a huge hotel with a lobby which reminded Dana of a railway station. Its name meant "town in heaven." During the afternoon she visited many of the booths where proprietors were selling colored stones. This was an ideal place to purchase many stones because of Thailand's preferred-nation status and cheap labor force.

Preferred-nation status is used by many developed countries (e.g., the United States) to help developing nations (e.g., Thailand, Burma, Malaysia, India, Israel) improve their financial or economic condition through export trade. In effect, it provides for the duty-free importation of a wide range of products from certain countries which would otherwise be subject to customs duty.

Since she was shipping the stones back to the U.S., Dana was very careful to include the commercial invoice and a Form A with each parcel. To avoid switches, she wrapped the gems in white paper which had her signature on various spots. She then sealed the paper with Scotch tape.

Some of the merchants smiled when she used her Geiger counter on the colored gems. One asked, "Do you think my stones came from Hiroshima?" He laughed.

In total, Dana purchased two heart-shaped emeralds, one heart-shaped ruby, two heart-shaped sapphires, three oval sapphires, two oval rubies, four round rubies, two imperial topaz, and a large amethyst. She thought, "A good day. If I can do as well in Burma and Hong Kong, this will have been a productive buying trip."

Due to flight schedules, Dana arrived in Rangoon two days before the Burmese Jade Emporium. She had to obtain a seven-day visa since the emporium extended beyond a four-day visa.

Dana was sure the Burmese government arranged for the extra period in order to get more hard currency. She had brought enough mosquito coils and had purchased a carton of 555 Dunhill cigarettes and two bottles of Johnny Walker red label whiskey at the Bangkok duty-free counter. She exchanged one bottle for some kyats with the taxi driver on her trip from the airport to Inya Lake Hotel. She was worried about her supply of mineral water.

Since Burma Airways flies at random, Dana did not dare risk a trip away from Rangoon. She ate an excellent Burmese meal at the Karaweik Restaurant her first evening in Rangoon. This restaurant is located on the eastern shoreline of Royal Lake, and from a distance it looks like a large boat on the lake. While waiting for the Burmese dancing show, Dana took some night photos of the Shwedagon Pagoda. The golden dome at night was gorgeous as it seemed to rise from the far side of the lake. Later Burmese dancers performed on a large stage with a large banner proclaiming "Tourist Burma Welcomes You to The Golden Land."

The next morning Dana noticed a piece in the *Guardian,* a newspaper slid under her door. Under the headline "Kachin Insurgents Come Under Attack," she read these paragraphs:

> The Burmese army has launched a major offensive against the rebel Kachin Independence Army (KIA) in the far north of Burma. More than 10,000 government troops are engaged in the largest offensive ever against the KIA, which has been fighting since 1961 at the start of the "Burmese Way to Socialism" campaign.
>
> The target of the offensive, which began on January 30, is the KIA's main stronghold in the southeastern Kachin State, adjacent to the China-Burmese border. Troops are advancing rapidly toward Pa Jau, headquarters of the KIA's political wing, the Kachin Independence Organization (KIO). The KIO has played a leading role in Burma's rebel movement. Sketchy reports indicate that

45 government troops are dead and about the same number of rebels have been killed. At least two helicopters are missing along with their crewmen. There are scattered reports that the KIA has attacked government positions in other areas of Burma.

The second day was spent by Dana reviewing the jade stones. Although she did plan to bid on some of the jade stones, she also wanted to visit the various showrooms. She especially wanted to buy some pigeon-blood rubies, which were unique to Burma. Later, Dana planned to fly back to Hong Kong and purchase some jade for her shop.

The next morning auctioneer U Win Pe began the auction. He was a smiling, bespectacled Burmese who had conducted every Emporium since 1964. He announced the first lot in fluent English and the gambling began. Each buyer began writing his or her name and bid on a sheet of green paper, then folded it and placed it in a silver bowl. To the highest bidder went the brown rock or boulder.

* * *

Frank Harrison had a direct American Airline flight from Philadelphia to Tucson. Since travel was a deductible expense, he was in the first-class section. The Tucson Gem Show in February was the major event for colored stones buyers in the U.S.. Frank drove to the airport via Interstate 95. The direct link to the airport from the Interstate was constructed in the 1980s, and since then travel to the airport had become much more convenient. To the right, Frank could see the Philadelphia Sports Complex and to the left the Food Distribution Center as he passed the Broad Street exit on the Interstate. Frank enjoyed going to ball games at both the Spectrum and Veterans Stadium. Just this past weekend he had watched the 76ers beat the Celtics in basketball on Saturday, and the Flyers beat the Canadiens in hockey on Sunday. Frank's favorite place in the sports complex was John F. Kennedy Stadium. Although a virtual white elephant today, it had hosted the annual Army-

Navy football game for over a half-century, drawing crowds in excess of 100,000 people. As a child Frank had often attended the game prior to its relocation across the street at Veterans Stadium.

As Frank approached the Schuylkill River, which is the dividing line between South and Southwest Philadelphia, the Philadelphia Naval Base was clearly visible on this cold, clear morning. One of his favorite historical sites, Admiral Dewey's flagship, was located there. Also visible to Frank were the many oil refineries located along the Schuylkill River. The proximity of the Schuykill River to the Delaware River made the location advantageous for oil refineries since oil barges could navigate the waters with relative ease.

Frank felt fortunate that he was able to find a place to park so close to the airport terminal. He made sure he wrote down exactly where he was parked and walked briskly to the terminal. It was one hour and fifteen minutes until his flight. "Plenty of time to write and mail a note to Janet concerning some work to be done at the jade shop," he thought to himself.

Frank walked up to the airline counter to get his boarding pass. He was greeted by a cheerful, sandy haired, tall young man of about 28.

"Yes, sir, what can I help you with today?"

"I'm traveling to Tucson," Frank replied as he pulled his ticket out of his coat pocket and presented it to the clerk.

"Do you have any luggage to check?"

"No, thank you." Frank always avoided checking baggage if possible. Not only was he concerned about the possibility of the luggage being lost, but he could not stand waiting for the luggage to be unloaded from the plane.

The clerk began to flex his fingers over his keyboard and looked at a monitor. "Would you prefer window or aisle?"

"Aisle."

"Smoking or non-smoking."

"Smoking."

"One moment, sir."

Frank began tapping impatiently on the counter with his fingers. The airline clerk looked up and Frank could tell by his expression that something was amiss. "Mr. Harrison, I'm very sorry, but the smoking section of the plane is completely full in first class."

"Can't you increase the number of rows?" a worried Frank inquired as the thought of a four-and-one-half-hour flight without a cigarette caused him to perspire.

"No, sir, first class is completely full on this flight." The clerk paused and added, "If you want I can check if there's any room in smoking on coach."

"Yes, please do that." Frank did not enjoy flying and the thought of doing so without a cigarette caused his worries to intensify.

"Coach is full in the smoking section also. Maybe someone would be willing to trade with you since you have a first-class ticket. There's really nothing else I can do, Mr. Harrison."

"Fine," Frank grumbled, obviously distraught. He gathered his carry-on luggage and headed toward his gate. Once seated at the proper gate, he began writing instructions to Janet.

1. Discount note receivable from Brown at bank.

Frank began calculating. It was an $8,000, 6%, 120-day note so it had a maturity value of $8,160. Frank's concentration was temporarily broken by an attractive woman of about thirty who was sitting by herself. Frank started to straighten his tie and comb his hair. Before he could walk over to her, she was joined by another guy who was obviously either her husband or her boyfriend. "Just my luck," Frank muttered to himself.

Frank resumed his calculations. "Let's see," he said softly with a sigh. "Maturity value $8,160, bank discount rate of 9%, bank will hold the note for forty days, so $8,160 times 9% times forty divided by 360 days in a year equals $81.60." Frank subtracted the $81.60 from the maturity value to come up with the proceeds equaling $8,078.40. Frank added to his note to Janet:

1. Discount note receivable from Brown at bank. You should receive $8,078.40 in cash.
2. Make entry in books. Debit cash $8,078.40, credit interest revenue $78.40, credit notes receivable discounted $8,000.

Frank paused and smiled before deciding on adding the following:

> The note receivable discounted account is a contingent liability. That is, if Brown does not pay the maturity value of the note, then the jade shop must.

Frank chuckled as he thought of the prospects of Brown reneging on the note. Pulling out his Texas Instruments pocket calculator, Frank began calculating the cost of the bond he had purchased for the jade shop as a long-term investment. It was a $5,000, 8%, five-year bond that was bought at 102 plus two months of accrued interest. Frank calculated the accrued interest by multiplying the $5,000 by 8% and then multiplying that total by the number of months of accrued interest (which is two) divided by the twelve months in a year. This process converts the annual interest to two months of interest. The accrued interest equaled $66.67. Since the bond sold at 102, that means that it sold at 102% of its face value. The total cost plus accrued interest totaled $5,166.67.

3. Record purchase of long-term investment in bonds. Debit long-term investment in bonds $5,100, debit interest receivable $66.67, credit cash $5,166.67.

Frank addressed an envelope, enclosed the note and mailed it to Janet at the jade shop. "Downtown Philadelphia gets two deliveries a day," Frank reasoned, "so the latest she would get the note would be tomorrow."

"Will passenger Frank Harrison please report to the ticket counter at gate 19."

Frank walked over to the counter after hearing his name paged. He wondered if there was an emergency with his consulting business that required his immediate attention. He hoped that it wasn't something which might affect his travel plans. "I'm Frank Harrison," he said with a bit of anguish to the young lady behind the counter.

"Mr. Harrison, we've had a cancellation and we are able to seat you in the first-class smoking section, but I'll need your ticket and previous boarding pass to make the switch."

"Terrific!" Frank gave her his ticket and boarding pass and received his new boarding pass. After thanking her for her trouble, Frank breathed a sigh of relief, sat down, opened his briefcase, and began reading his latest issue of *Management Accounting.* "Today's going to be a good day after all," he thought to himself as he lit up a cigarette in celebration.

* * *

Fred Brown left Honolulu on Singapore Airlines. Soon he would be crossing the international dateline and he would lose a day. He always wondered, if a person's birthday fell on the missed day, did the person not grow one year older? "Maybe that's the reason for Gary Hart's discrepancy in his age," he chuckled.

Fred considered himself to be one of the toughest men alive. He had been one of the Navy's SEALs — an acronym for Sea Air Land Team. This is an elite group of about 1,500 Navy personnel who carry out missions under water, on beaches, and into harbors in enemy territory. Fred had been one of the 13 sailors who crept ashore on Grenada in Reagan's war with M-16 rifles strapped on their backs. They were sent in early to determine what the American forces would find when they landed.

His next adventure caused Fred to recall his training on the sand-colored compound in Coronado, California. Just down the bay from San Diego, Fred had undergone some demanding and punitive SEAL training. A five-mile swim against the Pacific Ocean currents, a 14-mile overland run and mountain-climbing exercises in full combat gear had been routine. Fred had become proficient with at least eleven different combat weapons and an expert at detonating a wide range of explosives such as limpet mines, cratering charges, and Bangalore torpedoes. In 24 weeks he had gone through parachute jump school at Fort Benning, Georgia, and had learned how to kill a sentry, abduct someone, and sink a ship.

Created in 1962 by President Kennedy, the SEAL force looked for physical and mental toughness. Fred remembered what his commanding officer had said. "Our first criterion is a man's confidence in his ability to achieve and a tremendous determination to excel. You need an inner spark, a special kind of motivation to overcome all adversity, regardless of what is put in front of you." Fred would need this inner spark for his latest Rambo-type goal.

Fred Brown was a Philadelphia developer; Brown Construction, Inc., was one of his several corporations. He opened a folder and began reading the operating instructions for a new laser cutting machine his company had recently bought:

Carbon Dioxide Laser Machine

> A revolutionary "sky-wars" breakthrough in our resonator cavity provides a lightweight cutting torch. Weighing only 48 pounds, our continuous-wave laser cuts large metal structures. It is excellent for large metal beams.
>
> Lasers have two important advantages over conventional tools. First, a laser beam does not get dull or change its size and shape as a result of wear. Second, its

performance is not substantially affected by workpiece hardness or machineability.

The CO_2 laser produces an invisible beam of light whose wavelength is 10.7um. and generates many kilowatts of power. The CO_2 uses a precise mixture of three gases (carbon dioxide, helium and nitrogen) for high power output operation.

The laser works by sending streams of energy through the chosen material, thereby causing sub-molecular particles within it to jump from level of activity to a lesser one (i.e., the material degenerates rapidly). Searing a path through 10 feet thick titanium at a rate of 20 feet per minute is quite possible. Obviously, careful control is necessary. It should only be used when connected tightly to a stable work bench, with the beam aimed into a large lead box. The beam is designed so that it will not penetrate lead.

The lead box also traps and thereby protects the operator from any toxic metal fumes produced by the cutting process. Protective eyeglasses and gas masks are suggested for continuous use, however.

Metal Engineering Company
8761 Pete Rose Way
Cincinnati, Ohio 45209

Fred would certainly test the laser machine for performance and workpiece hardness on this trip. Enough of that. Fred turned his attention to another closely held corporation. Browright International had done quite well importing rubies and investing in publicly traded stocks of regional companies. The company had been incorporated in 1980 by himself, the then up-and-coming national politician Jim Bright and his wife, and Frank Harrison.

Fred had received 30 percent of the par value common stock; the politician and his wife, 45 percent; and Frank Harrison, 25 percent. Although the term *par value stock* has become somewhat obsolete, they had issued par value stock to each stockholder. No-par stock most often has a stated value and is non-assessable (i.e., creditors may not hold the stockholders liable for any difference between the consideration given for the stock and its par value). The company had not repurchased any stock back from the stockholders so there was no treasury stock.

The problem was threefold. First, recent tax law changes had made the corporate form less advantageous. There was still the advantage of corporate limited liability, but a corporation was taxed twice — once at the corporate level and again at the stockholder level. With reduced individual tax rates and effectively higher corporate rates, the flow-through entities such as partnerships and S corporations were quite popular. A Subchapter S corporation was still a real corporation, but under the tax law there was no corporate tax. Since Fred did not wish the unlimited liability of a partnership, he was seriously considering the S election.

The second problem was less manageable. Some newspaper reporters were checking into the operations of the closely held corporation. Fred had refused to return calls to about six different reporters last week. He pulled out a newspaper clipping from the *Wall Street Journal* and reread parts of it:

> House Speaker Bright's dealings with mysterious Browright company revive questions about his ethics and judgment. The closely held corporation remains somewhat of a mystery. Its president, Fred Brown, would not return our phone calls and a three-day stakeout at his apartment yielded no results. A next door neighbor indicates that "I have never seen the gentleman, but he does get a lot of phone calls." The corporation lists its mailing address as a post office box in Philadelphia.

> Browright is responsible for much of Mr. Bright's financial success, but the treasurer, a Frank Harrison, indicates that "I have never asked the speaker for a favor." Mr. Harrison is a well-known financial consultant in Philadelphia.
>
> Browright doesn't have to disclose its dealings. Instructions issued by the House Ethics Committee, however, tell members to disclose underlying holdings of such investment corporations, but Rep. Bright doesn't.

Third, Bright's wife had recently complained about her return on her investment in Browright. True, they had not declared any dividends, but the earnings-per-share figure for the corporation was exceptional. Earnings per share is the corporation's net income per share available to its common stockholders calculated as follows:

$$\text{Earnings per common share outstanding} = \frac{\text{Net income} - \text{Preferred dividends}}{\text{Weighted average number of common shares outstanding}}$$

Browright had no preferred stock, only common stock. Even though Bright and his wife had received few cash dividends, the income was being accumulated in the Retained Earnings Account. In a corporation, income increases an account called retained earnings, and dividends reduce retained earnings. "Maybe we can declare a stock dividend to stop her from complaining," Fred mused. Stock dividends present the illusion to the stockholder that he or she is receiving something, but in reality the corporation sacrifices no assets. The Retained Earnings account is reduced by the market value of the stock dividend, but Common Stock and Additional Paid-In Capital are increased by the same amount to reflect the increased issuance of common stock. Thus stockholders' equity is unaffected by a stock dividend, although its composition changes. "Such a ploy just may be the solution to Mrs. Bright," Fred reasoned.

Since the Browright problem could not be solved now, Fred returned the clipping to his leather briefcase and withdrew a gold Cross pen and a yellow legal-sized writing pad. He drew a line down the center of the front page and across the top of the left side he wrote *Bangkok* and across the top of the right side *Chiang Mai.* Under the caption *Bangkok* he began listing:

1. Steel/chain nets
2. Steel cables (4)
3. Rope (300 ft.)
4. Shotguns (2)
5. Rifle (1) plus scope
6. Shells
7. Hunting knives (2)
8. Machete
9. Chisel
10. 2 large suitcases

Under the *Chiang Mai* caption he wrote:

1. Canteens (2)
2. Backpacks (2)
3. Snake bite kit
4. First aid kit
5. Mosquito repellent
6. Axe
7. Mess kit
8. Hammer
9. 50 cartons of cigarettes
10. Hat, jeans, bush shirt
11. Iodine
12. Matches (waterproof)
13. Food and water
14. Sleeping tent

15. Sleeping bag
16. Waterproof coat

Then at the bottom of the page he wrote the word *have* and listed the following items:

1. Jeweler's loupe
2. Sneakers
3. Compass
4. Night binoculars
5. Lightweight bullet-proof vest
6. Cutting torch
7. Pocket knife
8. Calculator
9. Protective eyeglasses (2)
10. Gas masks (2)

He thought about but did not write down the word *pistol.* As a safety precaution he had packed his brown polymer pistol in his suitcase. It had a ceramic barrel insert and six springs — the only metallic parts. The remainder of the pistol was made of plastic. It would escape detection from most security detection machines, but Fred had decided not to carry it on his person.

The weapon was a non-metal assassination pistol issued in the early eighties by the Soviet Union for KGB agents. Not until 1986 did the U.S. government Office of Technology Assessment admit:

> "From our investigations it appears that the materials technology does exist to produce non-metallic firearms whose only metal components may be some small springs."

Fred put his list back into his briefcase and pulled out a batch of 8-by-10 photos. He looked slowly at each of the colored photos. On the back of each photo was written *north, south, east,* or *west.* Approximate distances were written on a number of them. Fred took a felt pen and drew a horizontal line across the top of one of the pictures between the Banana Bud and the Hti on the Shwedagon pagoda.

Fred knew that the Shwedagon or Golden Dagon pagoda was the most celebrated object of worship in all of the Indo-Chinese countries. The site of a depository of a relic of Buddha, legend indicates religious activity at Shwedagon as early as 588 B.C.

When Fred's plane landed, the passport agent at Don Muang Airport in Bangkok was as thorough as usual. He took Fred's passport and observed him closely. He compared Fred with his photo — tall, bald, some black hair along the sides of his head, and a small black mustache — not quite as pencil-thin as Chicago insurance billionaire W. Clement Stone. The agent consulted his computer console for about two minutes, stamped Fred's blue passport and handed it back to him.

Once Fred was waved through customs, he met Cimi Kiengsiri in the airport lobby. They spent the remainder of the afternoon purchasing the supplies needed in Bangkok. They began the drive to Chiang Mai around 6:00 in the evening. Cimi drove steadily for about seven hours, stopping only for gasoline. Fred was able to sleep much of the way. He awoke at 1:20 when Cimi pulled into the parking lot of a small motel.

After a needed rest, Fred and Cimi purchased their remaining supplies in Chiang Mai. Cimi's four-wheel-drive Nissan was now full (including the rack on top). Fred strapped on his holster and inserted his plastic pistol. With their rifles and shotguns within reach, Cimi began the drive up Route No. 108 toward Mae Sai. Fred again slept, awaking only when Cimi came to a stop at the end of the road. They saw Jake and another Shan tribesman with three mules in the shade of an apple tree.

Jake's partner had red lips, almost like lipstick. Fred knew that many Burmese chewed a nut of the areca palm as a mild intoxicant. This habit causes bright red lips.

It took about 45 minutes to load the mules and hide the Nissan off the road by covering it with bushes. Cimi took the distributor cap with him. Fred covered himself with mosquito repellent and the four men began the trek north toward the Burma border. They reached Mae Sai around nightfall and slept in a grass hut. By sunrise the next morning the caravan had crossed the border into Burma — the golden land.

CHAPTER 11

> I recently heard a CPA remark that the only accounting principle which the Internal Revenue Service regards as "generally accepted" is "A bird in the hand is worth two in the bush." Although my friend overstates his case a bit — quite a bit — I cannot dismiss the thrust of his comment without some soul searching.
>
> — Sheldon S. Cohen,
> Commissioner of Internal Revenue

Lenny was feeling depressed. He was getting nowhere with the dean in trying to clear his name. It seemed that every attempt he made to reach Bob Hawkins was futile. In addition, his reputation had been tarnished. His consulting activities were falling off — especially among those who were Wharton graduates. Lenny was so preoccupied with trying to clear his name, that he ignored Dana's problems altogether. They had spent some time together around the Christmas holidays, but aside from that time, he had had virtually no contact with Dana for the past few months except by phone. He had felt very guilty when Dana called him last week to tell him that she would be going to Burma. He made a promise to himself that he would place a higher priority on trying to uncover Dana's cash-flow problems.

"Hey, Doc! Get a load of that guy!" exclaimed Woody, pointing to a teenager with green and orange spiked hair.

Lenny chuckled softly. He was treating Woody to lunch downtown. As they walked to the restaurant, Lenny was going to stop off at Dana's shop. Dana had told him that she would leave a key for him in an envelope with Janet. This way Lenny could go in and work at his convenience. With Frank out of town also, Lenny felt that he could make better progress.

"So you're thinking of leaving Penn for another school?" inquired Woody as he interrupted Lenny's train of thought.

"I really don't have much choice, Woody. Unless I can clear myself with the dean concerning my book, they will fire me," said Lenny in resignation. "Someone slipped a note under my door indicating that I was receiving Senator Biden's Award for Uplifting Research."

"Where are you looking to go?"

"If it wasn't for Rebecca being in school I might look outside of the area, but I don't think I'll leave the area, so I guess that means I'll talk to Villanova, Temple, and Drexel."

"It won't be the same if you leave," proclaimed Woody.

"Thanks," Lenny said as he smiled.

The two grew silent as they approached Sansom Street. It seemed to Lenny that for the first time both were seriously thinking of the possibility of Lenny leaving. Lenny had been at Wharton for quite some time. It felt comfortable to him, and he was used to the people there. The prospect of leaving made him uneasy over the uncertainty of it all. To a degree, Lenny felt that he was being tested. In less than two years his wife had died, and his career had been jeopardized. He could not help but feel that fate was dealing him a bum hand.

As they approached the jade shop, Lenny's train of thought was broken. They both entered the jade shop breathlessly. The cold winter day and the high winds that arose between many large office buildings in downtown Philadelphia often made extended walking difficult during the winter.

"Hey, they got some nice stuff in here," whispered Woody to Lenny as they both removed their gloves and unbuttoned the top buttons of their coats.

"I'll only be a minute, Woody. Why don't you look around?" Lenny suggested as he left to pick up the envelope from Janet.

"Yeah, maybe I'll buy out the place," joked Woody.

Lenny exchanged pleasantries with Janet and picked up the envelope from her. He then walked into Dana's office where he opened up the envelope and read the note inside.

Dear Lenny,

Enclosed you will find keys to the shop (#1 and #2), the office (#3), the desk (#4), and the files (#5 and #6). With Frank gone next week, you should have the opportunity to get a great deal done.

Please cheer up. Things are bound to get better for you. I am confident that you will be able to get the plagiarism charge settled at school. Take care of yourself.

Dana

Lenny put the keys in his trousers pocket and placed the envelope in his briefcase. He left the office, waved good-bye to Janet and joined Woody in the front of the shop.

"I hope I wasn't too long, Woody," Lenny said apologetically.

"That's fine, Doc, but there's something over here I want you to see."

"You're finally starting to appreciate the finer things in life such as jewelry, is that it, Woody?" joked Lenny.

"Look over there," ordered Woody, pointing to a locked glass case at the end of a counter just in front of the display window. "Isn't that the same squirrel we saw at the warehouse that night?"

Lenny looked, and sure enough, it appeared to be that same hideous greenish-colored squirrel eating a nut. "It looks the same to me," replied Lenny.

"You can't forget anything that ugly," said Woody.

"I wonder how much it costs," said Lenny curiously.

"You're not thinking of buying that, are you?"

"I'm just curious, Woody."

Lenny motioned to Phillip, who had just finished waiting on another customer. "Yes, sir, what can I help you with?"

"I was wondering how much that squirrel in the case here costs."

"One moment, sir. Let me look it up." Phillip walked over to a large black book which had the prices of all the merchandise in the store. After turning several pages, he returned to Lenny and Woody.

"That squirrel is made of some of the finest jade known to man. It sells for $6,500. I know it is expensive, but from what I understand, the jade it is made from is exquisite."

Woody began to protest. "$6,500! Why, that squirrel is — "

"Quiet, Woody," Lenny ordered. "It seems to me that $6,500 is a fair price." Lenny turned to Phillip. "I want to think about it; I'm wondering if you could hold it for a couple of hours for me so I can make up my mind."

"Since you are a friend of Ms. Scott's, I don't think it will be a problem," Phillip replied.

"Are you crazy?" Woody asked.

"Come now, Woody. Thanks again," said Lenny, turning to Phillip. Lenny was anxious to get Woody out of the jade shop as quickly as possible.

Once they were outside the shop, Woody stopped walking and said to Lenny, "Have you lost your senses? Don't you remember that we saw that squirrel in a box marked imitations?"

"I sure do," said Lenny with a smile.

"Then why in the world are you going to pay $6,500 for that thing, and why are you smiling?" questioned Woody.

"Woody, my friend, I think I've just figured out how Dana is getting ripped off."

"How is she getting ripped off?" inquired Woody.

"I don't have all the details worked out yet, but if my guess is correct, Fred Brown is selling imitation jade to Dana and passing it off as authentic. I'm going to have to look at the invoices to make sure."

"How does this Harrison guy fit into it?" asked Woody.

"I don't know, but he may be getting a take on the profits with Brown on the imitation items sold to Dana," mused Lenny. "As soon as we've finished lunch I'm going to see what I can find out about it."

"I think I'll give you a hand," suggested Woody.

"Woody, you've got to go back to work."

"They'll never know I'm gone," countered Woody. "Besides, I haven't seen you this excited in a while. I also want to make sure that you don't buy that stupid squirrel."

Lenny laughed. He had to admit to himself that for the first time in many weeks he felt enthusiastic. This discovery was the first positive breakthrough in trying to uncover Dana's cash-flow difficulties. He wasn't really interested in eating; he preferred to go to work on Dana's books.

Lunch was indeed short, and within half an hour, Lenny and Woody were back at Jade and More. First, Lenny looked for the invoice on the squirrel. He found it after going through the Fred Brown file. He was surprised to see that the squirrel was marked as being received and inspected by Dana. He expressed his surprise to Woody.

"Do you think that she thought it was authentic or do you think that she sells phony merchandise to people?" Woody inquired.

"I don't know, Woody. Maybe this is a legitimate squirrel even though it came from Fred Brown."

"I'll bet you a beer it's fake," Woody challenged.

"I'm going to find out," Lenny replied. He walked out of the office into the front of the store where he spoke to Phillip about buying the squirrel.

"I've decided to buy the squirrel," Lenny proclaimed to Phillip. "Is it possible for me to pay for part of it with my American Express card and be billed for the rest?"

"I don't think that will be a problem under the circumstances," replied Phillip. "You will have to fill out this form indicating the terms of payment and your agreement to abide by the terms."

It took Lenny about ten minutes to fill out the form. Phillip put the squirrel, which weighed about ten pounds, in a carton and wrapped it with paper. While Phillip was doing this, Lenny went back to the office and told Woody that he was going to go out for about thirty minutes. Woody said he might take a little nap while Lenny was gone.

Lenny opened the phone book to look up an address and left the office after writing it down. He then picked up the squirrel and left the store. He walked about halfway down the street and went into Irv's Jewels. It was a shop owned by Irv Moskowitz, whom Dana had mentioned to Lenny as someone whose expertise concerning jade she trusted.

Lenny explained to the clerk that he wanted to get an appraisal of the item he had just purchased. The clerk took a look at the squirrel and informed Lenny that he would have to see Irv Moskowitz, who was the expert.

Irv Moskowitz walked over, looked at the squirrel, and said to Lenny, "I hope you don't mind me saying this, sir, but if you bought this squirrel you have lousy taste. Make sure you keep that covered up when you leave; otherwise people are liable to think you bought that here."

"It belongs to a friend," Lenny replied with embarrassment.

Moskowitz put on his glasses and placed a bright light on the squirrel. He then rubbed his hand along the surface of the squirrel and began to shake his head. "This is one of the poorer examples of imitation jade I've seen. It's probably worth a little over $200."

"Are you certain?" asked Lenny.

"Well, it's a quick examination, so I may be off one way or the other by as much as $50."

"So the maximum value of this squirrel would be no more than about $300?"

"If you were in a dark room and the customer was drunk, you might be able to get $300 for it," answered Moskowitz. "Do you mind my asking how much it cost?"

"$6,500."

"I will say a prayer for you tonight, sir, or for your friend, because you were taken. Do you mind my asking you where you bought this thing? I ask you because most jewelers do not like to see our image as honest businessmen damaged by a few unscrupulous dealers," explained Moskowitz.

"It was bought at Jade and More," replied Lenny.

"Jade and More!" Moskowitz said in astonishment. "This is something I will bring up with the proprietors, sir, because I know them and I am confident that they will refund your money."

"Thank you, sir; how much do I owe you?" inquired Lenny.

"I think I speak for the rest of the proprietors on this street in saying that in good conscience I could not charge you for such an obvious injustice."

Lenny thanked Moskowitz and headed back to Jade and More. It was clear that anyone with any degree of expertise would recognize that the squirrel was not genuine. The only question in Lenny's mind was whether Dana was trying to swindle people, and how that could possibly create a cash-flow shortage. He decided that he wanted to look at the inventory list that Dana had completed a few weeks ago.

When Lenny returned to the office, Woody was sitting on a chair fast asleep. He woke up immediately when Lenny shut the door.

"Where have you been?" Woody asked.

"I went to get the squirrel I bought appraised."

"You paid $6,500 for that?"

"I'll get my money back, don't worry," explained Lenny.

"How much was it worth?"

"$300."

"You owe me a beer," Woody countered. "What's next?"

"I want to check the inventory records to see what items are not moving."

"Why is that?"

Lenny sighed as he walked over to a filing cabinet. "If some items are not moving, it may be because they're imitations."

Lenny gave part of the list to Woody and instructed him to place a check mark beside every item on the list which was purchased six months ago or more. Altogether, there were 412 items included in inventory that were at least six months old. Of the 412 items, 383 were purchased from Fred Brown.

"It looks like the business is being flooded by phony stuff from this Brown character," observed Woody.

"The next thing to do is to look up the invoices on these items and to see if Dana signed for them," commented Lenny.

Lenny pulled out the Fred Brown file and began to look for the invoice number which was on the inventory list. Woody checked out the signature on each one and marked off the item on the inventory list. After about an hour and a half they were finished.

"Well, Woody, what are the results?"

"The dame's name is on each one," responded Woody.

"How were you able to go through them so fast?" Lenny wondered.

"At first it took a little while to find her signature," explained Woody. "Then I found a shortcut."

"A shortcut?"

"Yeah, let me show you." Woody grabbed about ten invoices and held them up to the light. "You see, you can look through all the invoices and see that the signature matches on each one."

"Let me see that," Lenny said. "Those signatures are almost identical."

"See what I mean?" retorted Woody.

"But Woody, they are *too* identical. They look like they are traced. Woody, that's it! Frank has been forging Dana's name on these things."

"Maybe he forged your writing on that guy's paper," suggested Woody.

Lenny looked at Woody. "That would explain everything. Let's make sure."

"How are you going to do that?" asked Woody.

"First, I've got to find something else with Dana's signature on it besides these invoices. Let's see, there's got to be something around here." Lenny began opening up some of the drawers in Dana's desk to find some type of document to compare her signature.

"Here's some," said Woody as he pulled some papers from underneath the desk blotter.

"Let's see," Lenny said, taking the papers from Woody and comparing the signatures to those on the invoices. "No, these are the same," muttered Lenny as he handed them back to Woody. "Wait a second, I have a letter from Dana where she gave me the keys." Lenny compared the signatures and seemed relieved when he said to Woody, "Just as I thought. These are not the same. They are similar, but not the same. Frank Harrison must be forging Dana's signature on all types of documents. No wonder she's in the dark about so many things."

"I'm curious about something, Doc," Woody wondered aloud. "What does a jade shop have to do with a helicopter and maintenance uniforms?"

"Woody, what are you talking about?" asked Lenny with a smile on his face.

"Those letters I gave you were about renting a helicopter," explained Woody. "I can't figure out what they have to do with jade."

"Let me see them," demanded Lenny. He started to read the two letters, each on Jade and More letterhead.

Cimi Kiengsiri
1087 Chaiyapoom Road
Chiang Mai, Thailand

Dear Cimi:

I wish to thank you for the recent guided tour of the Burma border and setting up the meeting with the Shan tribesman — Jake. I will certainly have a need for your services in the future.

During the first week of February you shall meet one of my associates, Fred Brown, and take him to meet the same Shan tribesman — Jake. Also, on your next trip to the Burma border, please deliver this letter to Jake.

For your troubles I am enclosing a $50 bill. Thank you. I shall be in Bangkok during the first week of February.

Sincerely yours,

Dana Scott
Jade and More

DS:
Enclosure

Lenny was perplexed. There was nothing wrong with the first letter. But the second letter was a shock.

Jake,

This letter confirms our prior agreement. Please attempt the following:

1. Locate a medium or heavy-lift helicopter for use during the first week in February in Rangoon. A Puma or Chinook is fine. But a CH-53, CH-54 Skycrane, or Russian Mi-10 would be best.
2. The helicopter must be fueled.
3. What is the diameter immediately below the Banana Bud? What material is that portion made of (i.e., iron, marble)?
4. We need two maintenance uniforms.
5. You shall meet my associate, Fred Brown, on the Thai side of the Burma border during the first week of February. You know the spot.

Please confirm receipt of this letter. I shall be in Rangoon during the same week — Inya Lake Hotel.

Sincerely yours,

Dana Scott
Jade and More

DS:

Lenny looked at Woody. "Tell me, Woody, where did you find these?" he asked as he held up the letters.

"I got them underneath that blotter on the desk."

Lenny picked up the blotter and found a metal key and a sketch. He immediately recognized that the drawing was that of a pagoda which he had seen while in Rangoon, Burma. Dana was in Burma at the moment, but Frank was in Arizona. The entire scenario did not make any sense to Lenny. "What type of key do you think this is?" Lenny asked as he handed the shiny key to Woody.

"It looks to me like one of those keys for a locker like the type they have at the bus station or the airport."

Lenny looked at the key again. It had the number 289 imprinted on it. "There's only one way to find out, Woody; let's go."

The bus station was the closest to the jade shop. The bus station was a rather depressing place. It was well lit, but was occupied by many street people and drunks who sought refuge from the cold. Lenny walked over to the ticket agent.

"May I help you, sir?" the ticket agent inquired in a disinterested tone.

"Yes, I am interested in your lockers," replied Lenny.

"Five dollars a day, with one day in advance," the agent stated without even looking up at Lenny.

"No, I was interested in whether you had a locker number 289."

"We only have sixty lockers, sir."

"Thanks for your time." Lenny walked over to Woody and they headed to the train station, which was closer than the airport.

"I'll bet you a beer that it's at the airport," observed Woody.

"Why is that?"

"Whenever you look for something, it's always at the place you look at last."

"Woody, I would take you up on the bet, but we're practically at 30th Street Station, so it wouldn't make sense to go directly to the airport."

Located on Market Street between 30th and 28th Streets, 30th Street Station was a magnificent structure complete with sculptures, busts, and paintings. In addition to providing train service to suburban Philadelphia, 30th Street Station is a stop for the Amtrak lines along the Northeast corridor.

Lenny double-parked his car on the Market Street side of the station and walked into the busy train station. He found the information window where an elderly man in his sixties directed Lenny to the desk where lockers were rented.

A cheerful young lady in her twenties greeted Lenny at the desk. "Can I help you with a locker, sir?"

"I wanted to know if this key is the key to any of your lockers," Lenny replied. He held up the mysterious key.

The young lady took the key and frowned as she examined the number. "I don't believe so, but let me check." She began to turn around a spindle behind her which was full of keys. "Here we are. Number 289." She removed a worn key from the hook marked 289 and compared it to the metal key Lenny handed her. "No, sir, yours is a different key. You see the stem and teeth on your key are much larger than those on ours."

Lenny took the mystery key from her and said, "Thank you for your trouble." He headed back to the car where Woody was waiting. "It looks like you won the bet, Woody. It's not at the train station."

"We better get going, Doc. A cop stopped about five minutes ago, and he said if we were still here when he returned, he would write a ticket."

There was an entrance ramp to the Schuylkill Expressway adjacent to 30th Street Station. Lenny turned onto it and headed to the airport. After a fifteen-minute drive, Lenny parked his car, and together he and Woody went into the airport. They walked over to the information desk where they were directed to the person to speak with concerning airport lockers. The locker expert was a middle-aged man wearing a white dress shirt and a black tie with a name tag clipped onto his shirt. Lenny explained, "We are looking for the locker which fits this key."

The man examined the key and spoke to Lenny, "You are welcome to try, but none of our lockers have keys with teeth this big or with a stem as long as the one on your key." The man pulled out a different key and continued, "Our keys are generally much smaller — such as this." The man handed Lenny a key that was about half the size of the one with number 289 on it. "You are welcome to try your key on locker 289 if you wish. I'll have a security guard take you there."

The man spoke with a security guard, after which the guard walked over to Lenny and Woody. The security guard was a man in his early thirties who was slow and deliberate in his movements and conversation. He did not say anything of substance to Lenny and Woody, but the few words he did utter indicated that Lenny and Woody were not dealing with a future Rhodes Scholar.

Locker 289 was located at the far end of the Overseas Terminal of the airport. The guard pointed out locker 289 to Lenny and Woody and watched as Lenny unsuccesfully attempted to place the key into the lock. Recognizing that the airport was not the answer, Lenny and Woody quickly thanked the guard and headed back to their car.

"Any ideas, Woody? Where else in the city might there be lockers of this type?"

"Maybe it's for one of those lockers in a health club," suggested Woody.

Lenny paused for a moment and thought. "Maybe, Woody, it's not for a locker at all. What makes you think that it is for a locker?"

Woody sighed and replied, "It was just a feeling I had."

"Let's go back to my office at Penn and take a better look at this key."

"Fine by me," replied Woody.

"There was one good thing about this key not fitting a locker at the airport, though," stated Lenny casually.

"What's that?" Woody asked in surprise.

"You owe me a beer!" laughed Lenny. Woody joined in the laughter as they left the airport parking lot and headed to the university campus.

* * *

Lenny looked at his watch. It was now eleven o'clock. Woody was sleeping on the chair in Lenny's office, snoring away peacefully. Lenny walked over to him and shook him.

"Woody, why don't you go home and call it a night."

"What about you?" Woody asked between yawns.

"I'm going to leave soon."

"I still think you're crazy to be sticking your neck out for Dana. She may be guilty."

"No, Woody. Everything is too convenient. The signatures are too similar, and the letters were too easy to find. If she was trying to get away with something, I'm sure she would be more clever in concealing it."

Woody walked over to the doorway, put on his coat, and pulled his knit ski hat out of his pocket and placed it on his head. He looked at Lenny and said, "You may be right, but if she is supposed to be set up, why can't we figure out what the key is for? I'll see you later."

Lenny walked back to his desk. He felt that Woody had brought up a good point. Everything had been easy to follow. It was as if someone was leaving a perfect audit trail for him to follow, with the trail being artificially created to lead to Dana. Why did the trail stop now? There had to be some audit trail for the key; otherwise it wouldn't have been left there. The key to the riddle was a simple key.

Lenny was frustrated. He turned his attention to his unopened mail. He opened an envelope addressed to him, and was pleased to find a check made out to him for services performed.

"That's it!" yelled Lenny in his office. He felt ridiculous. "How could I have overlooked such an obvious audit tool," he thought to himself. There undoubtedly was a check written and recorded in the check register for whatever the baffling key was for.

Putting on his coat and grabbing his briefcase as he went out the door, Lenny got into his car and hurried over to the jade shop. There was virtually no one on the streets at this time of night, and Lenny was able to get there in ten minutes.

It wasn't long before he was poring over the check register, eyeing the column which indicated to whom the check was written in hopes of discovering what key number 289 was for. About forty minutes passed before he came up with a strong candidate. One week ago there was a check made out to the Hershey Hotel in Philadelphia. Key 289 could be a hotel room key.

Lenny knew that the hotel would not divulge the name of a hotel occupant or what room that person was in, so he decided to call the reception desk and ask for Dana.

"Good evening, Hershey Hotel," the voice said over the phone.

"Yes, could you ring Dana Scott's room for me, please. I believe it's Room 289."

"One moment, please."

It seemed like an eternity to Lenny before the gentleman returned to the phone. It was only about one minute before he did return, however.

"I'm sorry, sir, but Ms. Scott left strict instructions not to be disturbed under any circumstances. Would you like to leave a message?"

"No, thank you," replied Lenny.

Lenny immediately got his things together and headed for his car. He was definitely going to find out what and who was in Room 289.

The hotel was only a couple of minutes away. Lenny parked his car and went directly to the elevator, ignoring the plush and elegant lobby. He pressed the button for the second floor, feeling embarrassed that he didn't just walk up the steps.

Room 289 was at the very end of a long hallway. It appeared

from the outside that it could be a suite. Ignoring the late hour, Lenny knocked on the door. There was no response. He knocked one more time, but again there was no response.

Lenny took the mystifying key out of his pocket and slowly placed it in the keyhole. It fit! He turned the key slowly while looking around, and opened the door. Inside was a large suite of two bedrooms and a wet bar. In addition, there was a briefcase with Dana's name on it on a table and a set of luggage on the floor.

The suite looked as if it had been unoccupied for a few days. Not a single item was out of place.

Lenny wondered if Dana was really staying at the hotel. He called down to the front desk to try and find out.

"Front desk."

"Hello, would you send me some additional towels for Room 289? I just got back from my trip, and there are no towels in my room."

"Immediately, but are you sure you mean 289?"

"Yes, I returned earlier than expected," replied Lenny.

"You will have your towels in five minutes, sir."

Lenny walked around the suite. No clothes were hung in the closets. No toiletries besides those of the hotel were in the bathroom. Nothing except a Gideon Bible and the Philadelphia area phone book was in the dresser drawers.

A knock on the door interrupted Lenny's silent investigation. He walked over and opened the door, where a young man in his late teens wearing a red uniform with brass buttons handed him four sets of towels.

"We're very sorry, sir, for the inconvenience, but we didn't expect you back until the end of next week."

"Well, I guess I surprised you by my early arrival," said Lenny as he gave the young man five dollars for revealing that information. "Thanks so much for coming."

Just as Lenny had suspected, no one had been in the room for a few days. He walked over to the luggage and opened it, but found nothing but women's clothing and lingerie. Nothing suspicious there, he thought. Then Lenny decided to open the briefcase. The first thing he found was a one-way ticket to the Bahamas. It was dated for the day after Dana was to return from the Far East. He put the airline ticket aside and was horrified to find a folder which had written on it SHWEDAGON PAGODA.

Suddenly Lenny knew. Dana was going to rob the pagoda of its many jewels.

CHAPTER 12

> Despite its roller-coaster history, the Burmese people are convinced no lasting damage can befall the Shwedagon. Whenever the pagoda has been endangered, generosity has restored it to an even greater glory.
>
> — "Insight Burma"

Lenny made a decision. He had to go to Burma and try to stop Dana. Was she truly involved with this scheme to rob a religious shrine? Could he stop her? How? Or was Frank setting her up, as Lenny suspected, to take the fall by leaving incriminating evidence in Dana's name? Did he have time? He would have to act fast. He hurried to his university office.

Lenny looked at his watch. It was ten in the morning when he arrived at his office. He had been up since six the previous morning, working all night with canceled checks and the check register at Dana's office. Lenny took a look at himself in the mirror. He looked like he had been awake all night. He was badly in need of a shave and he had a ragged look to him.

Lenny called his housekeeper and explained to her that he had to go to Thailand for several days. "Please try to explain to Rebecca when she gets home from school. Tell her I love her."

Next Lenny called his office manager and told him that he would be gone for several days. Lenny kept a small suitcase at his university office packed with several shirts, two pairs of pants, and underwear. It was not unusual for him to spend the entire night working in his office when he was particularly interested in something he was working on. He added his black toiletry kit and his passport, closed and locked his suitcase, turned out his office light, and locked his office door. He walked outside and caught a cab to 30th Street Station.

He took an Amtrak train to Washington, arriving at 1:15 P.M. Lenny felt fortunate that he was able to get an hour of sleep on the way to Washington. He felt much more refreshed. A cab ride took him to 2300 Kalorama Road NW to wait in line at the Thailand Embassy. Within an hour, he had a visa for Thailand. Another cab took him to 2300 S Street NW. There he was lucky. Even though it was past noon, the Burmese Embassy promised to have his visa by tomorrow noon. Still another cab ride to National Airport and Lenny bought a plane ticket for Bangkok, leaving at 1:25 tomorrow.

With nothing else to do, Lenny caught a train back to Philadelphia. He spent some quiet time with Rebecca. Although he was exhausted, Lenny slept restlessly. He was worried, and did not know what he was going to do once he got to Thailand.

Lenny took Rebecca to her school on Tuesday morning and then took a shuttle flight to National Airport. Lenny was waiting at the Burmese Embassy at 11:10. As promised, Lenny received his visa before lunch, and then rushed back to National to catch his Northwest flight. After a 28-hour flight via Seattle, a sleepy and tired university professor landed in Bangkok. Lenny had been able to sleep only about two hours. He fell asleep in a comfortable chair in the Bangkok airport while waiting for his Thai flight to Rangoon.

* * *

"The next lot is number 546 — "

"Dana!"

Dana heard a familiar voice call her name at the same time someone touched her on her shoulder. She looked over her left shoulder and was startled. There was Lenny, standing in the Soviet-built Inya Lake Hotel in Rangoon, Burma.

"What, uh, what are you doing here?"

"I need to talk to you now. Can we go outside?" Lenny asked quietly.

"Sure. I'm not really bidding on any of this jade. Why are you here?"

"We'll talk outside."

Dana followed Lenny outside to the porch. Dana noticed that Lenny's clothes were wrinkled, and he looked quite tired.

Lenny placed his suitcase on the top stone step and then sat down. He faced Dana with an angry, gunmetal stare. He did not know how to start.

Dana bent down and kissed Lenny on his right cheek. "I am really glad to see you." She then sat down, giving Lenny a quizzical look.

There was an uncomfortable silence, but finally Lenny asked in a somber voice, "Are you involved in a scheme to rob the jewels from the Shwedagon Pagoda?"

Dana looked stunned. "Are you kidding me? How would I do such a thing?"

In a soft voice, Lenny tried to explain. "While I was auditing your records, I found copies of some letters underneath your desk blotter. You sent one letter to a person named Cimi. You arranged for a helicopter — "

Dana put her fingers on Lenny's lips. "Slow down. You're making this up, right? Are you writing a novel?"

"Look, Dana, I found the letters on *your* desk. You are here in Burma. It cannot be an accident that you're here. How did you expect to get out of Burma? They would have captured you in Thailand."

"Read my lips, Lenny. I know nothing about such a crazy scheme. Someone must have put the letters on my desk. I'm not so dumb as to leave incriminating evidence on my desk of all places. I don't even lock my drawers. Were the copies signed by me?"

"Yes." Lenny observed Dana frown when she heard this. "In fact," Lenny continued, "these letters are only a part of the puzzle. Detective Calhoun thinks that you tried to kill me."

"Kill you? You merely got mugged."

"What about the room in the Hershey Hotel?"

"Hershey Hotel! What about the Hershey Hotel?"

"The room at the Hershey Hotel with your three suitcases of clothes, and tickets to the Bahamas."

"I have no idea what you are talking about," insisted Dana. "Tickets to the Bahamas? I'm sure I wouldn't forget about something like that."

Lenny began to smile slightly. Dana had passed his test. He was convinced that she was not behind any scheme to rob the Shwedagon Pagoda. He reached over and kissed Dana and said, "I missed you. Let me tell you the sad story. On Monday morning, a friend of mine, Dr. Charles Ross was killed in my university office. Someone put a Russell's Viper in my desk and Charles opened it. I found him dead in my office — the snake still there. It was intended for me."

"A Russell's Viper," Dana repeated. "I saw one of those in Thailand. They are so vicious that they will attack to kill without aggravation. Frank was there also." Suddenly the color drained from her tanned cheeks. "Frank knows how deadly they are, and he would have the connections to obtain one. And he doesn't like you."

Lenny nodded in agreement. He then explained to Dana how he suspected that Frank was working with Fred Brown to steal from her. He mentioned the forged signatures he had found, the letters, the sketch of the Shwedagon Pagoda and the plan to rob it, and the hotel room.

"The way I figure it," Lenny confided to Dana, "Frank must be framing you for the theft of the gems on the Shwedagon. I know he went to Tucson, but there is no way of knowing that he is still there. I spoke to Janet before I left. She has no idea where he is staying in Tucson. I called his firm, but they would not give me any information."

Dana interrupted Lenny's thoughts. "When is the theft going to occur?"

"Tomorrow night." Lenny scratched his forehead. "Maybe it does make sense. The letters indicated that you would meet

Fred Brown on the Burma-Thailand border. Suppose Frank and Fred Brown are working together? You are their scapegoat. Frank probably put the snake in my desk because I might discover how he was taking the cash out of your business."

"What can we do?" asked Dana.

"First we probably should report what we know to the U.S. Embassy. Do you know where it is? What was his name? We met Robert Samson when we were here. We'll talk to him."

"The taxi driver should know. There's several over there." Dana pointed to her left. "Most private taxis are remnants of 1950s American cars. The government-owned taxis are newer Japanese models."

Dana and Lenny took a Nissan truck. The gray-haired Burmese driver with an angular face smoked a cheroot while changing gears and dodging packed buses, old pickup trucks, and ancient, creaky autos. Along the disintegrating sidewalks Lenny saw men wearing plaid sarongs, and there was a blaze of saffron from the robes of the many monks.

Lenny had forgotten that Rangoon stood neglected and forlorn. General Ne Win and his successor had managed to transform one of the wealthiest nations in Southeast Asia into the most economically pathetic country.

The cab jerked to a stop at 581 Merchant Street, in front of a crumbling, British colonial architectural building. Lenny slipped the cabbie two $1 bills. Inside the U.S. Embassy they were confronted with an attractive receptionist and a khaki guard with an M-1 rifle — both Burmese. There was also a U.S. marine guard nearby.

"May we speak to Robert Samson?" Lenny asked in a rapid voice.

With an exaggerated sigh, the receptionist turned and replied, "Do you have an appointment?"

"No, but it's extremely important that I talk to Mr. Samson at once. I'm Professor Lenny Cramer, a U.S. citizen, and I have information about a potential major robbery here in Rangoon."

"You probably should contact the police. Here, let me give you their address."

"Please, Miss, this is a delicate, diplomatic problem. Is Mr. Samson here? Please give him my business card. Tell him it's urgent."

The receptionist said something in Burmese to the guard, took Lenny's card, and walked through a door on her left.

She came out shortly and said, "Mr. Samson is not here and Ambassador Brighton is extremely busy, but he'll see you tomorrow at 10:30."

In desperation Lenny exclaimed, "Please tell Mr. Brighton that I believe that an American citizen is going to rob the jewels from the Shwedagon Pagoda tomorrow night."

Without a word the petite lady turned and went back into the room. Within 30 seconds a distinguished-looking man came striding out of the office, extended his right hand and said, "Dr. Cramer, I'm Felix Brighton. Please come to my office."

Lenny shook his firm hand and turned toward Dana. "Mr. Brighton, this is Dana Scott. She is with me."

Brighton smiled at Dana and said, "Nice to meet you, Ms. Scott. Won't you come in also?"

Dana and Lenny followed the ambassador into the modest office. Lenny was the first to speak. "Mr. Brighton, it's a long story, but we believe that a Fred Brown and Frank Harrison are going to rob the Shwedagon Pagoda tomorrow night. They are Americans."

"How?" Brighton asked in a disbelieving tone.

"Probably with a helicopter."

"How do you know this?"

"A mugging, a Russell's Viper, auditing, and some letters," Lenny replied.

"Please explain," replied Brighton as he pushed the bridge of his glasses back into place.

Dana interrupted, "I own a jade shop in Philadelphia and I asked Lenny to review my books while I was in Thailand and Burma. My cash was disappearing from my business." Dana looked at Lenny and continued. "Since Lenny started auditing my records, he has been mugged and almost killed by a Russell's

Viper that was placed in his university office. In fact, another faculty member was killed by the snake. Apparently my partner, Frank Harrison, has developed a scheme to rob the Shwedagon pagoda. Someone — maybe my partner — placed some forged documents on my desk, which Lenny found, to try to frame me."

Dana stopped and looked at Lenny. Brighton looked up and asked, "Who is Fred Brown?"

Lenny held up his hand as if he were at a meeting. "We really don't know. I have tried to locate Fred Brown, with little success. I believe that Frank Harrison and Fred Brown have developed some type of accounting scam to defraud Dana's partnership. Fred Brown would not return the telephone calls I left on his message machine, and I have been unable to reach him at his apartment. As you can see, I believe this attack on the Burmese religious shrine will occur tomorrow night. What can we do?"

"This is a delicate matter. There have been some anti-American activities in Rangoon over the past two weeks. Our school for American children has been closed for two weeks. We have advised Americans not to go outside at night. This attack would play right into the hands of these rebels.

"The Burmese president demonetized most Burmese bank notes last month, which set off violent student protests. The army brutally crushed campus unrest in 1974. Are you staying at the Strand Hotel?"

"No, we are staying at the Inya Lake Hotel, Room 210. Why?" Dana asked.

"I need to check with the State Department. Since we have some time, I would rather not contact the police yet." Brighton looked at his watch. "It's early morning in the States. I'll call you late tonight or early in the morning. Have you eaten at the Karaweik Restaurant on the eastern shore of the Royal Lakes? If you haven't, let me suggest that you go there for dinner. When I learn anything, I'll call you there or at your hotel."

"That's great," Lenny said. "I haven't had a good meal in two days — at least it seems that long." Lenny suddenly felt tired and hungry. "Could we have your home telephone number?"

Brighton wrote his number on Embassy stationery and handed it to Lenny.

As Lenny and Dana were waiting for a taxi, Brighton sent two telegrams. The first was addressed to the U.S. State Department in Washington, D.C.:

> Urgent. Top Secret. Determine credibility of Dr. Lenny Cramer and Dana Scott, both from Philadelphia. Stop. Determine location of Fred Brown and Frank Harrison through passport control. Stop. Cramer and Scott reported a plot by Brown and Harrison to rob Shwedagon Pagoda by helicopter tomorrow night. Stop. Such an event would be a diplomatic disaster. Stop. Have all government agencies available to report any suspicious helicopter flights. Stop. Please advise me of the proper actions to take. Stop. Ambassador Brighton. End.

A second telegram was sent to the U.S. ambassador in Bangkok, Thailand:

> Urgent. Secret. Alert all military and political parties re potential plot by Americans Fred Brown and Frank Harrison to rob Shwedagon Pagoda in Rangoon. Stop. Alert Thai Coast Guard re helicopter flight from Thailand to Rangoon area. Stop. Ambassador Brighton.

* * *

A short telephone message originated from the U.S. Embassy. "Accelerate project. Plot uncovered. Local authorities not alerted."

* * *

Another Nissan cab took Lenny and Dana to the Karaweik Restaurant. Even at dusk, the temperature was still about 79 degrees, and yet February was the most agreeable month to visit Burma.

Approaching the restaurant, Lenny first thought it looked like a large boat beside the Royal Lake. He could see the Shwedagon across the wide Royal Lake, along with its shimmering reflection in the water. As the cab moved closer, Lenny realized that the concrete building had a double bow depicting a water bird. A many-tiered pagoda was on top.

Inside Dana remarked, "Look at the beautiful lacquer work on the walls. It's embellished with mosaic in marble, glass, and mother-of-pearl."

Lenny was so tired that he really did not enjoy the Burmese meal of rice, curry, and prawns. They drank Chinese tea rather than Burmese tea. From their table Lenny could see the towering Shwedagon from a window. Around 7:45 the floodlights on the pagoda came on. After eating, Lenny and Dana walked along a porch near the restaurant and the lake. "Look at the view of the golden dome on the Shwedagon. It's stunning. How do you think Frank is going to get the jewels off of it?" Dana asked.

"I don't know. I wondered about that on my plane trip here. I believe it is made of concrete or steel. Why don't we go over there now and check it out? I wonder who guards it?"

Dana didn't respond. She merely shrugged.

The only taxi they could find was an antique '57 Pontiac. Both Dana and Lenny were silent during the bumpy and noisy ride to the southern stairway on the Shwedagon Pagoda Road. Lenny gave Padah, the young driver, two dollars and then showed him a $10 bill.

"If you'll wait here for us to return, I'll give you the other half of this bill." Lenny tore it and handed one half to the driver. "Do you understand?"

"How long?"

"Oh, about 30 to 40 minutes."

"No problem," replied a smiling brown-faced Padah as he pocketed the torn bill.

At the stairway Dana asked, "Do you remember the last time we were here? One of the students counted the steps up to the main platform. Do you remember the number?"

"Really? How many?"

"One hundred and four."

As they walked up the stone stairway, they noticed that many of the stalls in the bazaar along both sides were closed or closing.

"There are a few old teak beams which survived the 1852 assault by the British," Dana said as she pointed to two of them.

About half-way up the steep stairs they crossed a concrete bridge. "At one time the pagoda moat crossed under this bridge," continued Dana.

At the top of the stairs were three guards. The human guard appeared to be asleep. The two other guards were mythological figures — a half-lion and half-griffin beast and a man-eating monster called an ogre.

The guard jumped up. He pointed to his watch, then to their feet. He spoke in Burmese. Dana looked at her watch. "We only have about 20 minutes. It closes at 9:00 and opens again at 4:00 A.M. Any attack against the stupa will probably occur between 12:00 and 3:00 — my guess," Dana suggested.

She began to take off her shoes and Lenny did the same. They walked on the inlaid marble slabs to the nearest of the eight sides of the gold-covered stupa. On each of the eight sides were eight smaller stupas.

Dana and Lenny stood for a few minutes observing the main pagoda, and then began walking rapidly clockwise around the octagonal base. "Buddhists always walk clockwise around their monuments," Dana said.

They walked quickly around the fourteen-acre plaza encircling the dome, stopping briefly at the northwest corner to observe the 23-ton Maha Gandha Bell. Lenny remarked, "The British tried to carry the bronze bell away in 1825, but it fell to the bottom of the Rangoon River. The Burmese were able to float the seven-foot-tall bell to the surface with bamboo poles."

Suddenly Dana asked, "Suppose they try to get the gems tonight? We haven't heard from the Embassy yet."

"Let me take you back to the hotel and I'll come back here and watch the place."

"No — not by yourself. I'll stay with you."

"It's too dangerous, Dana."

"I have too much at stake. Remember, the letters have my signature on them and who knows how many copies of those are around. You stay here, and I'll go back to the hotel and call Brighton. Then I'll come back."

On the ride back to the hotel Dana asked Padah, "How do you get gasoline? I thought gasoline was rationed at three gallons per day."

Padah laughed, "Only one thing runs smoothly in Burma — the black market. I can get gasoline on any side street for about $22 per gallon."

* * *

A Soviet-made Hind A helicopter slowly rose at a 10-degree angle from the Mingaladon Airport to hover status. The olive-colored helicopter had two swatter missiles and 128 rockets in four pods. In the cramped quarters the Burmese air-force pilot pushed the stick between his legs forward, raised the collective pitch lever on his left further up, and gave more pedal to balance the increase in torque as he made the transition from hover to forward flight.

Through the fragile, protective glass the khaki-uniformed pilot saw the floodlights on the golden dome black out as his aircraft entered balanced forward flight conditions. With many more moving parts, the helicopter was much noisier than a fixed-wing aircraft. His flight pattern would take the aircraft to the right of the stupa. The steady movement gave him a detached feeling of power over the darkness and the danger ahead.

* * *

Lenny was sleeping in the back seat of the '57 Pontiac. Dana had been able to only doze in the front seat, but the Burmese driver had been snoring for some time. At 12:40 Dana almost jumped when the floodlights on the golden dome went dark.

"Lenny, wake up," Dana said as she shook him.

Lenny opened his eyes slightly and grunted.

"The floodlights have gone out."

"What time is it?"

Dana switched on the battered flashlight and said, "About 12:40."

The flashlight or the talking awakened the driver, who said, "What's up?"

"Do they normally turn off the floodlights at night, Padah?" Lenny asked.

"Nothing is certain in Burma, but the lights most often are left on," Padah replied.

Lenny was silent for a moment and then said, "I'm going to walk up to the platform and talk to the guard. Try to keep them awake. Can I get out, Padah?"

Padah opened the car door, but no interior light came on. Padah opened the back door for Lenny — there were no inside door handles. Lenny pulled out his billfold, tore a $20 bill in half, and handed one piece to Padah. "Do not leave. You'll get the other half when I come back down."

A big smile came to Padah's face. "I won't leave, Doctor!" This night was a gold mine for Padah. Dana had given him a carton of cigarettes for the trip back to the Inya Lake Hotel. At Rangoon's Scott bazaar, a carton of cigarettes went for $45 at the official rate of exchange. Dana had promised to give him a bottle of Scotch when the night was over — worth $107 in the moribund economy.

Lenny went around the dirty Pontiac to get the flashlight from Dana, but she was standing outside with the car door closed. "I'm going with you." She had her binoculars.

Lenny knew there was no reason to object, since she would come anyway. They both walked across Shwedagon Pagoda Road to the Southern Stairway. A nearly full moon would help their walk up the 104 steps. All shops were closed. They could only hear their footsteps on the stone steps, and the small glow of the flashlight on the rough steps was eerie.

"Shhh-hh," Lenny said, as he put his hand on Dana's shoulder. They both stopped.

At first their labored breathing was the only thing they could hear. Then came the distinctive sound of a helicopter far in the distance. There was a sour feeling in the bottom of Lenny's stomach. "They may hit tonight. Brighton should have taken this more seriously."

They both began walking faster up the wide, darkened walkway. The floodlights were still off. As the erratic whirring sound of the helicopter became louder and louder, they walked faster and faster.

When they were about 20 steps from the top of the walkway the sound of the helicopter changed. Somehow both Dana and Lenny knew that the attack had begun. The helicopter was hovering somewhere near the Shwedagon platform.

When Dana and Lenny reached the top of the walkway, the sound of the helicopter was deafening. To their surprise there were no guards at the top of the walkway.

Their fears had come true. A helicopter with no lights was hovering immediately above the towering stupa. Two dark bodies were dangling from ropes, working around the top of the dark dome. Over the noise of the whirling blades Lenny could hear another sound — like a chain saw cutting through rock.

The dark bodies wore lights on their hats. They looked like coal miners in the dark. They wore gas masks.

Dana shouted into Lenny's ear, "Where are the guards or the police?"

Lenny shrugged. He saw a third man in the helicopter lower a net. Without thinking Lenny went running down the main platform to the base of the pagoda. The down draft from the helicopter made it difficult for Lenny to breathe. He began shouting, "Frank, we know that it's you!" The noise was so deafening that the people 300 feet in the air could not hear him, but the man in the helicopter must have seen Lenny running.

Once the net was in place, the man in the door of the helicopter pointed a gun at Lenny and fired. Lenny heard the bullet ricochet off of a smaller stupa beside him. He ducked behind the nearest structures. They were prayer pillars.

Lenny watched from behind the pillars. There was nothing he could do. He then began to see some monks moving from structure to structure, the rotor wash blowing their saffron-colored robes. The man in the helicopter fired sporadically at a moving figure.

Suddenly Dana darted behind one of the pillars. She shouted to Lenny, "Look through my binoculars. The lower figure looks like Frank."

At that moment the top part of the pagoda fell into the net and it was pulled into the helicopter. Another large net was lowered as the upper figure moved down to help the one below. They had cut the very top off and were working on the second portion of the towering dome.

Lenny stood up behind the prayer pillars to get a better look through the binoculars. He could not identify any of the thieves.

About three more minutes flew by, and one monk came into the open walkway shaking both fists at the invaders. The man in the helicopter shot, and the angry monk fell to the marble floor. Parts of his saffron robe slowly turned a dark red from flowing blood.

Suddenly both attackers began to push at the top portion of the dome. A second, larger piece fell into the net and was pulled toward the helicopter. The two bodies slowly turned beneath the helicopter, observing the chaotic scene below.

A policeman or soldier came up behind Lenny and Dana with an M-1 rifle. He stood up to aim his rifle at the helicopter. One of the turning figures pointed his machine toward the soldier and a pin-like light came through the darkness and severed a sacred bird on top of the prayer column. The debris fell on the soldier, as he ducked in fright.

As the two figures were pulled toward the helicopter, it began moving toward the northeast. The helicopter felt a little tail heavy, but slowly at first and then faster, it moved toward the dark horizon. There was an occasional rifle shot as the whop, whop, whop of the helicopter blades become softer and softer. Dana and Lenny could barely hear the whirring sound of the molester when the floodlights came back on.

The rape of the Shwedagon Pagoda was consummated — it had been denuded of most of its treasures. The towering golden dome was now flat on top.

CHAPTER 13

Profit is only a pious name for legal plunder. Debt is like morphine. How do you suppose that millionaires get the property they possess if someone does not first lose it?

— J. A. Wayland

Burmese troops soon appeared en masse. A few primitive Air Force prop planes could be heard overhead and mass confusion reigned. The old planes reminded Lenny of a Civil Air Patrol air show he had seen one year in Harrisburg, Pennsylvania. Padah, Dana, and Lenny were immediately taken into custody. Gunfire could be heard in the distance along with a loud explosion.

When the troops approached Dana and Lenny, Dana quietly whispered to Lenny that they should say nothing about what he had discovered in Philadelphia until Ambassador Brighton saw them. Lenny nodded in agreement, and the two of them refused to answer any questions in spite of repeated interrogation by military officials.

Lenny was physically drained. He was beginning to feel the effects of a lack of sleep. But the hard cot and the strong urine smell kept Lenny awake — or was it fright? He and Dana had been placed in separate cells after they were initially questioned about three hours before. Since that time, he had seen only two military officials, who asked him several questions. It was with great relief that Lenny saw Ambassador Brighton walk into his bare cell.

"Am I glad to see you!" Lenny exclaimed.

"I can imagine," Brighton replied cordially. "Tell me," he said in a low voice as he bent his head down towards Lenny's, "have you told any of these people anything you informed me about in our previous conversation?"

"No, Dana suggested that we not say a word until you arrived."

"Excellent," Brighton responded, his eyes widening. "Now I won't be too long, but when I return you just go along with whatever I say and hopefully you'll be out of here in no time. Do you understand?"

Lenny nodded in assent. "Good," replied Brighton. "I shall not be long."

Thirty minutes later, two heavily armed guards appeared. They ordered Lenny to come with them. The guards took him to the large interrogation room where he was relieved to see Brighton, Dana, and a man who appeared to be in charge of the military guards, considering all the metals he was wearing on his chest.

"Dr. Cramer," Brighton began as Lenny sat down at the end of a long table next to Dana, "I have assured General Kang that you are prepared to identify Frank Harrison as the man you saw at the pagoda, and that you are prepared to identify him as the mastermind behind the entire operation."

Lenny really had not seen Frank during the attack on the pagoda, but he remembered what Brighton had told him about echoing his words. "Yes, that is true," replied Lenny.

He glanced over at Dana. He saw her let out a long sigh of relief at his answer.

"With your permission, sir," Brighton said, turning to General Kang, "I will put out a nationwide alert for Frank Harrison within the United States, and will notify the Thai authorities about the possibility of Harrison being in that country at the moment so that they can alert their border patrols and customs agents."

The general nodded in assent. "Unless you have any further reasons for detaining Ms. Scott and Dr. Cramer, I will take them back to the Embassy with your permission," Brighton added.

"Permission granted," General Kang uttered in a deliberate manner.

Brighton shook hands with the general and motioned to Dana and Lenny to stand up. A guard returned Dana and Lenny's personal effects, including their passports. They then left the building with Brighton, climbed into a waiting air-conditioned Chevrolet, and headed to the Embassy.

"Luckily, there is a flight leaving Burma in ninety minutes," Brighton said sternly. "I have arranged for the two of you to be on it. I will have a member of my staff get your personal belongings at the hotel and send them off next week. The important thing for now is for you two to get out of the country as soon as possible."

Lenny turned and looked at Dana, but she was just staring out the window. He turned back to Brighton and said, "I feel that I should tell you that I didn't see Frank Harrison at the Shwedagon Pagoda."

"Sure you did," Dana interrupted. "Don't you remember my pointing him out to you?"

"I never got a real good look at him, though. They were wearing gas masks and miner's hats."

"This is precisely why you two must leave here immediately," said Brighton forcefully. "Now don't say another word about this entire incident until you are safely on American soil."

The trio continued on to the Embassy and later to the airport in virtual silence. The return flight to Seattle was uneventful. Lenny slept most of the time, and Dana was very reserved.

When the plane landed in Seattle, Dana told Lenny that she had some relatives she was going to visit in Seattle, and that she would see Lenny in Philadelphia in a couple of days. Lenny felt it was an unusual time for someone to visit relatives, but he was too tired and nervous to complain. He returned to

Philadelphia early in the evening and went directly home to get a good night's sleep.

* * *

When Lenny awoke the next day he just had enough time to say hello to Rebecca before she went off to school. He felt a little guilty that he had neglected to spend much time with her lately and made a mental promise that he would rectify that situation.

Upon arriving at Wharton, Lenny called the dean to make an appointment to try to hopefully straighten out the plagiarism charges with the new information he had about Frank Harrison being a forger. Lenny then related to Woody what had taken place while he was in Burma. Woody shook his head in disbelief.

Lenny looked through his calendar and found that he had a luncheon to attend in Cherry Hill, New Jersey, the next day. Lenny really did not feel like going, but it was sponsored by a group of CPAs in southern New Jersey, and it was a good opportunity for Lenny to pick up some consulting work.

Woody stopped by later in the day to see if Lenny wanted him to pay off his beer bet today. Lenny laughed and told him to forget about it. About an hour later the phone rang.

"Doc, this is Woody. I thought you would want to know that the FBI arrested that Frank Harrison guy today."

"Where?"

"At the airport. He just got off a plane from Arizona."

"That was a front, Woody. He went to Arizona, but he went from there to Thailand and from Thailand to Burma. I'm relieved they got him. I feel a great deal safer."

"They didn't say what he was arrested for, Doc. In fact, I've been checking the newspapers and none of them even mention the robbing of the pagoda."

"I think both governments are trying to keep it as quiet as possible because of the turmoil that could result in Burma — especially the possible anti-American activity."

Woody and Lenny spoke a little longer. Soon Lenny took off for home to spend a quiet evening with Rebecca.

* * *

Although Cherry Hill is in New Jersey, it is within thirty minutes of downtown Philadelphia and is in reality a suburb of the city. Cherry Hill is a town of many large single homes in clean, well-kept neighborhoods. It is also a town with several fine restaurants, a racetrack (Garden State Park), and many service industries which serve mostly suburban clients. Lenny found Cherry Hill nice and peaceful, but he preferred the bustling city life to that of the suburbs.

As a former president of the American Accounting Association, Lenny was seated at the head table. He was going to present a certificate of achievement to Charles Wengston for his work in establishing a drug and alcohol rehabilitation program for accountants.

Lenny was already seated at the table when a short blond-haired man of slight build sat beside him.

"Hello, I'm Lenny Cramer."

"Pleased to meet you. My name is Charles Wengston."

"I must congratulate you, Charles, on your work on alcohol and drug abuse. What got you interested in it?"

Charles smiled, "That's nice of you, Lenny. My interest really began back when I was an undergraduate at Pfeiffer College and a friend of mine was killed when he had too much to drink and drove into a tree."

Lenny's head shot up when he heard that Charles had gone to Pfeiffer College. "So you went to Pfeiffer College. A friend of mine went there also. She is about the same age as you, but I doubt if you would know her. She was in an entirely different field."

"Who is it?" Charles asked. "It's a very small liberal arts college, in Misenheimer, North Carolina. I may know her."

"Dana Scott."

"Sure. I know Dana Scott. She was the top accounting student my senior year. She was on the tennis team, and had an accounting assistantship. I remember how she scored in the high nineties in an Advanced Accounting exam and the next highest grade was in the seventies. I haven't seen her in years. With what accounting firm is she working?"

Lenny was stunned. "Are we talking about the same Dana Scott? About 35 years old. Attractive. Well built."

"That's the same one. Like myself, she was from New Jersey. We had quite a large contingent from New Jersey there at Pfeiffer."

"She was an accounting student?" asked Lenny in disbelief.

"The best in the school," replied Charles.

"Will you excuse me, please?" Lenny asked as he stood up and headed for the door. She's been putting me on all the time, he thought to himself. He thought back to his mugging, the Russell's Viper, and the accusations of Officer Calhoun that Dana was someone of whom he should be wary. A chill went down his spine as he walked to the bathroom.

* * *

Lenny went back to his office after the presentation. He had this horrible feeling that he was being set up. He gathered both the documents he had that contained Dana's signature and those that had what he previously had believed to be a forgery of her signature by Frank. He also found the three MBA cases that had been prepared by Robert Hawkins. He telephoned Officer Calhoun.

"You get those documents to me right away," said Calhoun with forcefulness, after hearing Lenny's fears about Dana and the ransacking of the Shwedagon Pagoda. "We'll run some handwriting tests on those signatures and analyze them immediately."

Lenny arrived at the police station thirty minutes later. He gave the documents to Calhoun and waited for the results. Calhoun had told him that it would probably take anywhere from two to five hours. In the meantime, Lenny told Calhoun in greater detail about the pillaging of the pagoda.

"I talked to a friend of mine in the FBI. He told me that at the moment the only evidence they have against Frank Harrison is the statement made by you and Dana Scott to Ambassador Brighton that the two of you saw Harrison at the pagoda," Calhoun informed Lenny. "Apparently he was in Arizona."

"I never saw Frank Harrison. Dana said she thought she saw him, but I didn't see him. Ambassador Brighton told me to go along with what he said in order for Dana and me to be released as soon as possible."

"The FBI also told me that they want the documents you brought in today. In fact, they are probably trying to get you now," added Calhoun.

Before Calhoun could continue, his phone rang. The analysis of the signatures was complete. It had taken only two and a half hours. Calhoun went to get the results, and told Lenny to wait until he returned.

Ordinarily Lenny would have found a police station fascinating. People of all walks of life come and go constantly. Computer terminals with access to files of criminals from all over the world were on many of the desks within Lenny's line of vision. Lenny observed none of this, however. Instead, his mind was on the signatures. Had Dana made a fool of him? Was he attracted to a thief? Had he unintentionally helped in the destruction of the Shwedagon Pagoda?

Calhoun walked briskly back into the room holding many of the documents which Lenny had brought to him earlier. He sat down next to Lenny and showed him the letter that Dana had written to him and signed before she left for Thailand.

"This document we know contains Dana Scott's genuine signature," said Calhoun. He then pulled out a purchase order for goods to be purchased from Fred Brown. "Now this purchase order to Fred Brown contains a signature that is very similar, but different from the one on the letter to you. The signature is made with a little less pressure, which can be detected in the thickness of the strokes. You can see it easier in this blown-up copy of the two signatures."

Lenny looked at the magnified versions of the two signatures. The differences were readily apparent. "I knew that she couldn't be involved," sighed Lenny in relief.

"Wait a second," cautioned Calhoun. "This third letter is the letter to the helicopter company. While the signatures are not identical, I think you can see that when magnified the signature is much closer to the one on the letter to you, Dr. Cramer, than on the purchase order to Fred Brown."

Lenny examined the magnified signatures. It was clear that the signature to obtain a helicopter was the same as the one on the letter to him. He looked at Calhoun with resignation, "I guess this means that Dana was involved."

"I really am sorry, Dr. Cramer," Calhoun said with sincerity in his voice. "I know this must be difficult for you. We also looked at the fingerprints on the documents, and we found that both your fingerprints and another set are on all three. We feel fairly certain that they belong to Dana Scott."

Lenny looked around the station awkwardly. He regretted not listening to Calhoun earlier or paying heed to Woody's warnings. He looked back to Calhoun and asked, "What happens now?"

"Prior to coming back here to show you the evidence, I issued an APB for Dana Scott's arrest. We hope to pick her up shortly."

Lenny chuckled weakly, "I guess that an APB in your profession does not stand for Accounting Principles Board as it does in my profession."

Calhoun smiled, "No, it stands for All Points Bulletin." He paused and continued, "I will let you know of anything that develops. We will probably ask you to make a statement after we arrest her. Also, we cannot tell from the photocopy of the Hawkins cases whether or not it's your handwriting. But my men will continue to work on it."

Lenny shook hands with Calhoun and headed out into the cold February air. Somehow, Lenny noticed neither the cold air nor the fine sleet which started to fall. His mind was totally blank.

* * *

"I won't be long, Rebecca. You just wait here in the lobby for me."

"I'll just read this magazine, Dad, but can't I go in?"

"No, you just wait here, and then we'll go out to dinner," promised Lenny.

Lenny walked to the visitation area of the minimum security facility where Dana was being held until her trial. It was three weeks to the day since her arrest. Her fingerprints were the ones which appeared on all three documents, as Calhoun had suspected. She had plea bargained to get a reduced sentence in exchange for testifying against Fred Brown. Lenny really did not want to see Dana, but he had so many questions which were unanswered. He had to get them answered.

The guard brought Dana to the visiting area. She looked very tired and pale to Lenny. She smiled weakly at Lenny and sat across the table from him. The guard sat off to the side at a point where Dana and Lenny could easily be observed.

"Hello, Lenny."

"Hi."

"How is Rebecca doing?"

"She is fine, thanks." There was an awkward silence. Lenny decided to pursue his main purpose for being there. "Thank you for agreeing to talk to me. You didn't have to."

"I felt I owed you an explanation," Dana said softly. "It all snowballed so quickly."

"Why did you get involved in this?" inquired Lenny.

Dana sighed before responding. "It all started when I came across the scam that Frank Harrision and Fred Brown were pulling on me. I found the purchase order where Frank forged my signature and saw that he and Fred Brown were stealing money from me by having Jade and More buy inferior merchandise from Fred Brown at top-of-the-line prices. I confronted Fred Brown with my findings."

"What did he do?"

"He told me about this elaborate plan he had to obtain the

treasures from the Shwedagon Pagoda. I guess I let my greed get the best of me. The plan was to let Frank continue to think that he was stealing money from me with the aid of Fred Brown. Then we were to pin the blame on Frank for the pagoda incident."

"So Frank wasn't involved with the taking of the pagoda at all?" queried Lenny.

"No."

"I heard that the plan didn't work out anyway because the helicopter carrying the top of the pagoda crashed."

Lenny wanted to move on to some items he was most concerned about, but he was not sure how to approach the subject. He decided to be direct about it. "Dana, I need to ask you about the mugging and the snake."

"You have to believe me, Lenny, when I tell you this. I had nothing to do with either one of those things. Frank was responsible for the mugging. He told Fred that he was concerned that you were going to uncover his scam. To appease Frank, Fred had one of his henchmen follow you and mug you on the way to your meeting with Fred Brown in order to discourage you from moving too fast in your examination of my books. I didn't know anything about it until after it occurred."

"And the snake?"

"I swear to you, Lenny, I was in Thailand when that occurred. I knew nothing about it. It was all Fred's idea. He was concerned that you might interrupt the pagoda operation. He knew that you were very able. He gave me his word he would not do anything to you, but he did this after I left."

"You knew how I was framed with the plagiarism charge, didn't you?"

Dana glanced at the guard and turned to face Lenny again uncomfortably. "Yes. Fred told me what Frank had done to you. I hope you will be reinstated. I knew that it was causing you some financial stress, but I felt that it was better than causing you physical harm."

"Thanks for giving me the lesser of two evils," replied Lenny sarcastically as he began to think of the lawsuit he was going to file against Frank for damage to his character. "There's one other thing I am curious about, Dana — why me? Why did you need me to be involved?"

"In order to place suspicion on Frank, we needed an outside party to discover that Frank was a scoundrel. We needed someone to determine that Frank was stealing money from me. An accountant was the best source. Neither Fred nor myself expected you to find the documents and the key under my desk mat, however. We felt that the police would find it and, with your help, arrest Frank."

"It almost happened that way. But wouldn't that at the same time place some suspicion on Fred Brown?" Lenny inquired.

"Think about it, Lenny. What did he do? Sell items at inflated prices to a willing customer. At worst he could be accused of fraud, but that would only occur if I pressed charges. After the snake and the attack on the pagoda, the police want him for much more, including murder."

"Where is Fred?"

"I really don't know," Dana answered.

Lenny's curiosity was satisfied. He stood up and looked at Dana. "I appreciate your agreeing to tell me all of this. I know you did not have to. I know things must be rather difficult for you at the moment. Thanks again."

"Lenny," Dana said in a low whisper as her eyes began to fill. "I want you to know one thing. I never did deceive you about how I feel about you. I hope that someday you will find it in your heart to forgive me."

Lenny thought about the mugging, the loss of a valued colleague, his running all over the city and all the way to Burma. He thought about witnessing the attack on the pagoda and the frightening time in custody in the Burmese prison cell. He thought about the false faith he had placed in Dana — a conspirator in the attack on the Shwedagon Pagoda. He thought of all of this before replying to Dana's plea. "Good-bye, Dana. I'm only glad you didn't hate me."

Depressed but relieved, Lenny walked out of the visiting

area. Rebecca was happy to see him, but could detect his obviously sad state. "Dad, I have an idea."

"What's that?"

"Why don't we plan on taking a trip overseas in the spring?"

Lenny turned quickly and saw from the smile on Rebecca's face that she was joking. They both burst into laughter and together walked out of the police station in a happier state of mind.

* * *

When Lenny returned home, for some reason he dialed Fred Brown's phone number. After the recorded message, Lenny gave his name and phone number, asking Fred to call him.

The next day Lenny's dean called and said, "Robert Hawkins is dropping his charge of plagiarism against you. You are officially reinstated in the School of Business. Please be more careful in the future."

Three days later an anonymous envelope addressed to Professor Lenny Cramer arrived at Lenny's university office. Inside was a clipping from a Bangkok newspaper:

> On Friday, government and religious officials celebrated the replacement of both of the stolen parts back onto the Shwedagon Pagoda. More than 200,000 people watched and cheered as the helicopters and workers repaired the damage done by three foreigners on this sacred shrine.
>
> A government official said that the two portions of the pagoda were found in Northern Burma unharmed. The many diamonds, rubies and other precious stones were still intact, including a 76-carat diamond. Apparently the attacking helicopter crashed in the jungles of Burma, after lowering the stolen parts into a deep ravine. The official indicated that three badly burned bodies were found in the helicopter wreckage. One body was believed to be that of Fred Brown, an American ruby dealer

affiliated with Browright, Inc. Fred Brown, a Philadelphia developer, has close connections with U.S. House Speaker Bright. Rep. Bright indicated that "All of my stock holdings are in a blind trust, and I have no knowledge of a Fred Brown."

A Buddhist leader stated that "Buddha has protected the Golden Pagoda once again. Neither man nor nature can take the legend from us." The Shwedagon Pagoda rose 326 feet above its base before the daring midnight attack on the shrine last week. In earthquake-prone Burma, according to legend, the glittering golden pagoda is 2,500 years old, but has been rebuilt many times.

On Friday morning, Lenny answered his phone. "Hello," he said.

"Dr. Cramer, you called me. This is Fred Brown."

Lenny was dumbfounded. "I thought you were dead. Wait a minute. There were four people in the helicopter. Right?"

"It is best that I remain dead. Thus, Dana will probably only get probation. So I suggest you forget any conversation that we may have. Do you understand?"

"How do I know you are Fred Brown?"

"Suppose I told you that I could have easily killed you with my laser device while you were hiding behind the prayer pillars. Remember the police ducking beside you and Dana?"

Lenny gained some composure and asked, "Was it worth destroying a religious shrine and killing an accounting professor?"

"That's why I'm returning your call. I had nothing to do with the Russell's Viper. That must have been Frank's doing. So if you wish to avenge your friend's death, look to Frank and forget about me."

"I'm curious; how much were the stolen gems worth?" Lenny asked.

Fred laughed. "I should have known better. If the Emerald Buddha in Bangkok is made out of jade, what could be expected on the Shwedagon Pagoda?"

"What do you mean?" Lenny exclaimed.

"There were no jewels on the precious pagoda. Does that tell you anything about the original Buddha hairs?"

"What happened to them?"

"Who knows? There was a minor earthquake in 1970, and the pagoda was clad in a bamboo scaffolding while it was being refurbished. The socialist government could have taken them at that time."

"There was a 76-carat diamond on it. Surely that did not just disappear?" inquired Lenny.

"I checked on that. The English Dresden is a 76.5-carat pear-shaped diamond that apparently is in India now. Remember, the British were in Burma and occupied the pagoda for two years after the First Anglo-Burmese War in 1824. Then in 1852 the British took and pillaged the pagoda for 77 years until 1929. The English Dresden was discovered in 1957."

"The British were involved," repeated Lenny.

Fred continued, "The Sierra Leone was cut from a 75-carat crystal found in Sierra Leone in 1959. It was eventually cut into a 32.12-carat pear-shaped gem. Then there's the Nepal Pink, a 72-carat, old Indian-cut, rose-pink color diamond seen in Nepal in 1959. The present ownership is unknown. Of course, General Ne Win took control of Burma in 1958."

"So it's possible that the gems have been gone for many years," Lenny interjected. "How did you get away?"

"Luck. We lowered the pagoda into a ravine, and I went down to check out the gems. A Burmese helicopter spotted our helicopter and started chasing it. Apparently it crashed and my three helpers died. I immediately began to dig out the stones. Most of them were zircons, garnets, quartz, glass, and junk. Someone else robbed the Shwedagon Pagoda, not me."

"What are you going to do?"

"Assume a new identity. I'll survive. By the way, Dana does like you. Do not try to find me. You'll only harm Dana. Got to go."

Lenny did *not* try to locate Fred Brown.